Mandy M. Roth

KING OF PREY

A Bird Shifter Novel

THE RAVEN BOOKS

King of Prey (A Bird Shifter Novel)
Cover art © copyright 2014, Andrea Depasture

King of Prey © Copyright 2014 by Mandy M. Roth
First Print Edition Publication February 2014, The Raven Books
Second Electronic Printing 2014, The Raven Books
First Electronic Printing 2006
ISBN-10: 1499635648
ISBN-13: 978-1499635645
Edited by: Angela James, Suz G. and Dianne B.

RAVEN
WWW.THERAVENBOOKS.COM

KING OF PREY
Mandy M. Roth

MANDY M. ROTH FEATURED BOOKS

King of Prey (Bird Shifter Series)
King of Prey
A View to a Kill
Master of the Hunt
Rise of the King
Prince of Pleasure
Prince of Flight

Immortal Ops Series
Immortal Ops
Critical Intelligence
Radar Deception
Strategic Vulnerability
Tactical Magik
Administrative Control
Separation Zone

PSI-Ops Series (Part of the Immortal Ops World)
Act of Mercy
Act of Surrender
Act of Submission
Act of Security
Act of Command

DEDICATION

In honor of my ten-year writing anniversary I've decided to expand and re-release some of my favorite books. *King of Prey* is one of them. It's hard to believe it's been eight years since I first put pen to paper to bring my bird shifters to life. Eight years since the other realm was born in my imagination and eight years since larger-than-life alpha male shifters swept in to claim their mates. I can't thank you all enough for being part of this journey with me. I hope you enjoy this expanded edition of *King of Prey*.

CHAPTER ONE

Accipitridae Realm

"King Kabril, you cannot stand idly by while your people cry out for you to lead. Our race will not survive unless you take a wife. The mating magik that governs our lands will not grant established unions the blessing of children if the leader himself refuses to sire offspring," Sachin said, his words the truth. As head advisor to the king he was afforded the opportunity to speak freely where others were not. It was a privilege Kabril was fast beginning to suspect needed to be revoked. "You know the laws, the way of the land and the demands you must meet as king. The time has come, my lord. This can wait no longer. The people of Accipitridae need you to act now."

Though Sachin's words were the truth, they were not what Kabril wanted to hear. No. He much rather preferred hearing all was well and that none of the people under his rule were troubled. Of course, those moments were few and far between of late. The rumbles of pending war continued to make their way through the kingdom. Now was not the time for foolishness or for stopping everything to heed the warnings of those who did not leave their chambers.

Ever.

Seers and the Oracle.

He grunted. He had no time time for prophecy.

It had been a good long while since his people had been in full-scale war. Yes, they had the occasional run-in with the enemy, but nothing epic. Too long for some to remember the horrors of it, yet not long enough for others to be afforded the chance to forget.

Kabril was one of the men who could not forget. He did not want a repeat, nor did he want his people's moods soured because he was refusing to do what was required of him as king. Gods be damned if what they required didn't go against his very nature.

Select a wife.

Settle upon only one woman—forever?

Absurd.

Truly, he would have thought it a trick of the Oracle had so many not stood behind the words.

Foolish words.

Sighing, Kabril leaned back on his throne and stared into the reflective mixture Sachin held in the bowl. He ran his fingers over the scrolled armrest and glanced down at the carved hawks. A slow smile caused by pride moved over his face. Pride in his people, their traditions and their beliefs, even though those very beliefs were the cause of his unrest.

He did not want to be forced to select a queen. Far too long he'd ruled alone, answered to no one and liked it just fine that way. He did not require the assistance of a female.

Few men did.

Females tended to talk too much and think with their hearts, not their minds. Such was a luxury men could not afford. He shuddered to think what would come to be should females ever rule the realm. There would be nothing but talk, talk, talk.

He nearly groaned at the thought.

"A curse on the prophecy," he muttered, making Sachin laugh. He looked to his friend. "They are wrong to put such stock in charms and magiks."

"At one point in your life, you too believed the seers to be true and wise."

He scoffed. "'Twas before I knew better."

"You are most difficult, my lord."

7

"I could have you beheaded," Kabril returned.

Sachin merely snorted. "You could try."

The people of his kingdom assumed their issues with conceiving were due to his reluctance to accept what they deemed to be destiny. Kabril wasn't a staunch believer in the gods or of prophecy as he should be, but it came from being the one forced to accept a wife he did not want. As their ruler, it was his sworn duty to do what was best for the kingdom, regardless how much it pained him.

"My lord," Sachin pressed, his reluctance to let the subject rest putting Kabril's already taxed nerves on edge. The man would not cease his endless prattle about the subject no matter how much Kabril deemed he do so.

Kabril knew. He'd tried to decree it law not to speak of the ordeal.

Sachin simply ignored him.

As was the norm.

Taking a deep, calming breath, Kabril reminded himself of how proud he was, and should always be, of his people's customs and beliefs. Although he was less than pleased with the Oracle—whom they held in such high esteem—choosing a bride for him. According to the prophecies, the Oracle would select a woman fit to lead his people, and he was honor-bound to obey. It was also said the union would produce children, something their kind sorely lacked. Once heavily populated, his lands were no longer bursting with the sounds of children singing and playing. In truth, Kabril could scarcely recall when the sounds indicative of children stopped, but he knew it had been far too long.

War had claimed the lives of many of his people. Still others, while immortal to a degree, possessed the ability to pass on to the afterlife should they so choose. There came a time in many people's lives when they were ready to move on. It mattered not what the cause was—their population was low, as was morale. Riches only did so much to calm the people. They wanted families.

"Cursed Magaious," he spat, not caring if he took one of the Epopisdeus' names in vain.

Sachin clapped acrimoniously. "Bringing down the wrath of the bird gods will surely ease your burden, my lord. For if you curse one, they all rise to strike."

"You push me too far, old friend." Kabril smoothed his fingertips along the wood of his throne, ignoring the internal nudge to free his temper.

"You do not push yourself far enough."

Kabril hated when Sachin was right.

Giving Sachin a daring look, Kabril let loose another curse upon the gods. He once again selected the god he knew Sachin honored weekly in hopes of provoking his friend. He was in the mood for a fight and Sachin was always a worthy adversary. The two often sparred until matins. Depending upon the day, Sachin would either continue the match or lay his sword down to go honor the gods. Kabril had long since given up his prayers to higher powers. "A pox on Magaious and those who follow him blindly."

Sachin merely tipped his head a little and released an exasperated sigh. "Remind me again which of us is older? You seem to be acting like a fledgling, my lord."

Arguing with Sachin would get him nowhere since it was clear Sachin was not going to take his bait. Damn him for being levelheaded. Kabril hungered for an argument, even a sparring match. Steel upon steel would settle the debate. For there was nothing more soothing than the clang of steel and the vibration up one's arm from a good strike and an equally as good counterstrike.

Sachin would obviously give in to neither. Kabril truly hated when his advisor was calm. It took all the fun out of a good fight. Kabril drummed his fingers on his armrests, trying to devise a plan for avoiding marriage.

Especially to a human female.

9

A ripple of disgust washed through him. He was king, not some peasant, and even he would not wish a human upon a peasant. He was not that cruel a king.

Why was it the Oracle seemed to favor reopening the portal to Earth? The prophecy only stated his need to find his mate. It never said she was an Earthling. It wasn't as if an Earth woman was fit to be queen of his people. Their species was substandard to say the least. They lacked the means to be anything but human.

Kabril shuddered. The mere thought of not being able to shift forms into that of a hawk and soar the skies nearly caused him to lose the meal he'd eaten to break his fast.

The very idea of relying on machinery to lift me into the sky. How repulsive.

Not only that, but humans were foul as well. Their entire world was polluted, overpopulated and riddled with disease. They took nearly no care with their realm and allowed men with gold-lined pockets to kill the planet, quicker, rather than slower, as if it did not matter to them that the gold would serve little in the way of burying all their dead.

The only thing Earth had less of than Accipitridae was conflict. His breed, the *Buteos Regalis*, had been at odds with the *Falco Peregrinus* for centuries. Longer than even Kabril could recall the reason why, and he was nearing his four-hundredth cycle, though he had only held the throne for one hundred and fifty of those cycles. They teetered upon the abyss of another war. He could sense it coming, looming in the distance, waiting for the right moment to strike.

What was will always be.

Glancing around the Great Hall, Kabril realized it had not changed much in the long centuries he'd ruled. Truth be told, not much had changed since his father was king. Kabril was not one for redoing what did not require being redone. But he did assure what was there was well cared for, disliking clutter or rundown states of matters.

Open saucers with floating wicks hung from the ceiling on chains of gold. The oil within them burned at a steady pace, and on occasion he would see brief flashes of a servant scuttling about to refill them. Those who made the castle function often tried hard to stay out of his line of sight, as if they feared the very glimpse of them would cause the skies to open and fire to pour down upon them. He was not so pompous as to believe a servant should never be seen. He appreciated what they did to keep things in order in the castle and often tried to reward them without their knowing that it came directly from him.

It would do no good if they thought him a soft king with too many emotions.

No.

Nothing was easy.

It never was.

He needed to relax, take time from the demands of the throne even if just for a day and then return to it all—clear of head. His demanding schedule had stopped allowing for rest periods some time ago and seemed to be brimful from morn until night. Part of it was his own doing. He disliked putting the burdens of running the kingdom upon anyone else's shoulders—though he had enough brothers to request assistance from. They did not hold much love with the idea of ruling and seemed almost grateful that birthright deemed he do so.

Lucky bastards.

He used to have something that resembled a personal life that he was permitted to live as he saw fit. It wasn't much because of the commitments of ruling the hawks, but it was his and his alone.

Seemed like forever ago.

CHAPTER TWO

Kabril sorely missed the days of roaming about freely, shifting shapes and soaring anywhere his heart desired. He preferred the Tocallie Mountains in the Northern Region of Accipitridae because of their isolation and beauty. Waterfalls cut through the large, foliage-covered terrain creating a serene and secluded paradise. He'd often heard Earth possessed such places of beauty and wonder but had never seen them with his own eyes, so he was skeptical.

The Tocallie Mountains were favored by him for another reason—it was one of the largest portals to and from Earth. A place where, over the years, many of the humans' flying machines entered from a spot on Earth they called the Bermuda Triangle. Though rumor had it that other spots fed into the Tocallie portal too. Additional portals throughout his kingdom served as gateways from other regions of Earth but none were as active as Tocallie.

As much as he disliked the humans and their flying machines, he did like to learn. Physics and medicine were two of his favorite areas of study—neither of which a king had any use for. Still, that didn't stop Kabril from seeking out new sources for learning. He had even gone so far as to hire tutors to instruct him on the ways of medicine and treating animals. While he could always resort to his magiks, it seemed more of a challenge to do it the way humans did. More rewarding as well.

Sachin cleared his throat, drawing Kabril from his thoughts. "My lord."

"What did I miss this time?" Kabril asked, already annoyed with the man.

A chortle broke free from Sachin. "Did the 'my lord' give it away?"

"Yes." Kabril cast a speculative glance at his long-time friend. "You would rather eat *flankscud* pie than *my lord* me. You show me no respect. You should fear me. Most do."

Sachin shrugged. "They are fools, for I know you."

Kabril cast a sideways glance at his lifelong friend. He should have selected anyone other than Sachin as a head advisor. Sachin was too headstrong.

Had you, you'd never trust them the same.

Sachin beamed. "You would not make it a day without me. Stop dreaming it so." He was right. Never one to refrain from disagreeing with Kabril, Sachin was a breath of fresh air in a sea of followers. "I was saying you should visit your soon-to-be bride and win her trust."

"Win her trust?" he echoed, afraid his hearing had gone awry. Surely this was a conversation just to get a rise out of Kabril. Sachin could not be serious. Why would it matter to Kabril if his bride-to-be trusted him? He had no plans to keep her. She was human after all.

Sachin's lips trembled. It was easy to see his personal guard and trusted friend found great amusement at Kabril's response. Sachin ran his hand over his black goatee and shook his head. "King Kabril, you must get to know the human, make her love you."

Shocked, Kabril jolted, almost falling off his throne. "Surely, you jest. Get to know *it*? Make *it* love me?"

"Perhaps we should begin with you not referring to your future wife as 'it'." Sachin turned his head and Kabril knew it was to hide his smile. The moment his friend was composed, Sachin touched the dagger on his side. It was a nervous habit of Sachin's. The man took great solace in the knowledge his weapons were close. His silver gaze landed on Kabril. "Tell me you were not planning on abducting your future wife."

"I was actually planning on sending you to fetch her. I've no desire to visit Earth." The very idea made his stomach turn. Sachin couldn't really expect him to travel to a realm full of heathens. No king would. At best he would linger near the Tocallie portal while he sent one of his other guards through with orders to procure books and other learning tools.

"I am sorry, but I will not go unless you accompany me, *my lord*."

"Do you dare to defy me?"

Sachin leaned down and grinned. "Kabril, do not make me knock your pampered arse from that chair. You can and will go with me to find your bride. You can and will get to know her. Befriend her even. You can and will get her to love you. If I can still tolerate you after all of these centuries, I am sure she will at least be somewhat fond of you."

"Sachin?" he asked, his mouth agape. "Cease your blathering."

"Do not *Sachin* me, *my lord*. And I will not cease my anything. I have known you all of my three hundred and ninety-five cycles. I am permitted to uncover your veiled eyes when called for." He assumed a posture of superiority and shook slightly. It took Kabril a moment to realize Sachin was laughing.

Unable to stop himself, Kabril joined him, laughing from the gut. It felt good to release some of the tension he had locked away. In truth, Sachin knew him well. He knew that being direct worked to a certain degree. He also had a knack for taking an opposing view on a matter only to get Kabril to argue the point, all the while agreeing with Kabril. "Very well. It may be best for me to learn a *few* Earth customs."

"Actually," Sachin said, "I have something better in mind. May I suggest you alert the advisors you will be on Earth for many moons? Perhaps Rossi should be contacted to sit in while you are gone?"

"You wish me to call one of my brothers home to rule while I am on Earth for many moons? Now I know you jest. It is clear you suffer from the pull of the moons, Sachin. Mayhap you should seek the counsel of an old crone." Since four moons orbited their planet, one so large it was seen even in waking hours, it was always safe to blame them for madness. And it was apparent Sachin was afflicted with moon madness.

Shaking his head, Sachin chuckled. "No, my lord. I do not jest and I have not been stricken by the moons. There is much work to be done."

"Work?"

Sachin grinned mischievously. "Ah, the king must learn to speak as humans do, without drawing attention to himself. He must also learn the Earthly art of wooing a woman."

Kabril cringed. Nothing called "wooing" could be good. "Leave me in peace for a bit."

"As you command," Sachin said as he walked in the direction of the outer hall. "I will alert the others of your departure."

Kabril sighed and put his head back, closing his eyes, attempting to wish away the prophecies. It did not work. The gods did look favorably upon him at the moment. He could not blame them. He'd taken their names in vain and had mocked others' devotion of them.

Served him right to have to go to Earth of all places. A just punishment indeed. Next, the gods would say he must reside there until they deemed otherwise.

He shuddered.

He kept his eyes closed, wondering what his woman looked like. Flashes of long dark hair came to him and his body instantly tightened. His cock stirred to life and he groaned, his hand going to the front of his trews.

There was a harem in place at the castle. He could summon forth women from it to alleviate the tension in his cock. But he did not. Instead, he untied the front of his trews and released his cock, knowing he would not be bothered again.

15

Thoughts and the tiniest of flashes of a woman returned to him. He could not see her face or make out much of anything about her. All he did know was the very idea of her hardened him more. He wanted to find her, sink into her depths and lose himself in her. But he would not tell Sachin that. No. His friend would find too much joy in knowing Kabril truly did want the woman—whoever she may be.

Even if she was human.

He squeezed his cock harder, his breathing rash as he pushed thoughts of her being human from his mind. He needed a good fuck. He'd put too long between them. Mayhap the moons had afflicted *him*.

That was the only explanation for his body lusting after a human, of all things. He pumped his cock, his thoughts lost on a woman he could not clearly see while his body teetered on the edge of bliss.

Kabril continued to work his cock until his ball sac drew up and his seed spilled forth and onto the floor. A servant would see to the mess. They always did.

Though, once, he'd learned his seed had been taken to the Oracle in hopes of figuring out why the birth rates in the realm had dropped so. It was then the foolish prophecy had been spoken.

Kabril's cock wilted at the thought of it all. He tucked it away in his trews and sighed. Sometimes he wished he had the freedoms his brothers had. None worried about ruling or the tasks that came along with it. Each lived a life outside of the castle, for the most part.

Rossi, the youngest of his brothers, tended to spend the most time within the castle walls, no doubt because he liked the free use of the harem. Keonae and Aeson were next in line to rule—being part of a set of triplets that included Kabril. He had beat Aeson out by mere minutes, making him king.

Often, Kabril would sit and wonder what life would have been like had he been the second of the triplets to arrive. He had not spoken with Aeson in more than two full moon cycles. Last Kabril had heard, Aeson was off in the human realm—again. Disobeying Kabril's orders. And

Keonae now resided among the humans. Something Kabril had considered forbidding but with Keonae's past and the heartache his brother had suffered, Kabril understood the man's need to fade away from all that was known, and simply exist. And his other brothers—two sets of twins—were heading up different regiments of Kabril's armies. Doing as duty required of them.

CHAPTER THREE

Earth, six weeks later…

Rayna Vogel lay in bed, her sheets pulled up tight around her naked form. Morning light spilled into her bedroom window and she turned her head, allowing it to wash over her face.

She stretched, thinking about the dream she'd had. It was a doozy. Her body still tingled. She'd been whisked off by some warrior man who seemed very out of place, almost medieval in a sense. He'd taken her to a castle, high in the mountains, and once there he'd rocked her world. So much so her inner thighs still spasmed with the aftereffects of his rockage.

She tried to think of what he'd looked like.

Handsome.

Striking.

All man.

With a hefty dose of alpha.

But she couldn't actually remember his face. Only his body—and what a body it had been. Every detail of his shape and form. Even down to the dimples on his backside. She'd never seen anything like his body in waking hours. And probably never would, since she'd dreamed him up and all.

She lay on her back, her gaze going to the ceiling. It was good to be home. She spent such little time there anymore that she'd nearly forgotten how good her bed felt. Too much time away on photo shoots.

The money was welcomed and she'd saved every penny she could, living a rather modest life.

She was totally alone now, no family to rely on, no close friends to speak of. Her chest tightened, tears wanting to come. She blinked them away, took a deep, calming breath. She wouldn't cry anymore. Not over this. Crying wouldn't bring her loved ones back.

Nothing would.

She'd only just reached a spot in her life where she was able to say goodbye to certain things. Her grandmother's home was one of those things. The time had come to let it go, to allow someone else to find joy there, someone else to perhaps start a family there and breathe new life into the old dwelling. She had plans to greet the new owners later in the day.

Rayna eased out of bed, the sheet sliding away from her naked body. She walked to the window overlooking the backyard, which connected to her grandmother's grounds as well. It would be sad to see the home go, but it had sat empty too long now.

Her fingers grazed the window, the sunlight warming them instantly. She closed her eyes, thinking back to her dream. She'd felt whole and complete when dreaming of him. If only that filtered into her waking hours.

"Time to turn over a new leaf," she said, taking a deep breath and turning from the window in the direction of her bathroom.

A long hot bath was in order. Then it would be off to try to make peace with giving up a large piece of her past. She just hoped she could hold it together when seeing someone living in her grandmother's house.

CHAPTER FOUR

Kabril dusted off his hands and looked around the location Sachin had secured for them. Supposedly, it was to be home for the duration of the fool's mission they were on. Kabril was not one to do manual labor. He had people for that sort of thing. Yet, for several weeks, he had put his time in, cleaning, de-webbing, and doing what he could to make the new dwelling feel like home.

As much as he wanted to punish Sachin, Kabril had to admit that doing things for himself felt oddly liberating. Of course, he would never tell Sachin such a thing. To do so would mean allowing Sachin to know he was right in forcing Kabril's hand and making him come to Earth's realm.

The home Sachin had selected from there was in close proximity to one of the portals back home. One near the Tocallie Mountains that Kabril favored so much. He'd given his word to try living among humans and not return to Accipitridae, but he was not sure he could actually hold true to his promise. The call of the mountains, of home, was simply too great.

"Considering breaking our agreement?" asked Sachin, walking into the room from the back hall, carrying yet another box. The old home seemed to posses limitless boxes, filled with what Sachin had explained were keepsakes, though they meant little to Kabril.

Kabril cast Sachin a warning look. "And if I am?"

"I shall mock you without mercy for centuries for being a coward."

"A what?"

"One without honor or bravery," returned Sachin. He looked very smug.

"I am dangerously close to killing you." Kabril touched his side, where he normally kept a sword.

"I know," said Sachin, setting down the box. "Why do you think I disarmed you upon our arrival?"

He opened it and withdrew something Kabril had learned was called a photograph. It was of an older human woman with a young one. The young one had long dark hair and huge wide eyes, a sharp contrast against her alabaster skin. She was stunning. Unlike any woman he'd ever seen before. Though, she was far too young for his tastes.

He looked upon the older woman more, soaking in the sight of what humans called aging. His kind did not age in a manner similar. It took them centuries before others stopped seeing them as too young, a mere fledgling. Human lives were but a blink of an eye.

"Sachin," he said, a serious tone to his voice. "When I meet this human who is to be my queen, I will not love her."

"Because you are incapable of such a thing or because you fear she will age and die?" asked his old friend.

Anyone else and Kabril would have leveled them for daring to question him on such a thing. But Sachin was different. And he was correct. Kabril touched the photograph, his hand running over the older woman. "They are fragile, are they not?"

"Yes, but the Oracle would not speak of a human as your mate if the woman was not as our woman are."

"Humans are not immortal."

"No," responded Sachin. "But stories of old tell of joinings between our kind and humans. Of how, once the claim was staked and the act followed through, that the human's life essence was then tied to the shifter's."

"Those are old tales told around campfires," Kabril said, worry lacing his heart. He did not want to love a woman only to lose her.

21

"There must be some truth in them, for long ago our ancestors did mate with humans." Sachin took the photograph from Kabril. "The young woman here is pleasing to the eye."

"Do not look upon her," snapped Kabril, taking it from Sachin and tucking it away beneath his arm. "Have you not something else to do? Perhaps more cleaning, as you have reduced us to the same rank as kitchen maids and serving staff."

"Oh, how the high born whine when they are forced to do something more than sit upon a throne."

Kabril pushed Sachin and hid his laughter as he walked away, keeping the photograph close to him as he headed up the stairs to the room he had claimed for himself. The young woman in it appealed to him greatly, though she should not. She was too young for him. Still, he would keep the photograph. It was the first thing since their arrival to earth that he found value in.

CHAPTER FIVE

Rayna Vogel stared at the old home, reminiscent of baroque styling, and smiled. It had been a long time since she'd seen the sculptures adorning the corners. Layers of dirt and webs had blanketed them to the point she'd long since forgotten how beautiful they were. Rayna had lived with her grandmother until it had been time for Rayna to go off to college. Even then, she'd returned and bought the home that had a backyard touching this one's. She had wanted to be close to her grandmother and still feel like an adult. Now that years had passed and so had her grandmother, Rayna realized how foolish she'd been. She should have just moved back home with the woman and been there in her final years.

Grandmother, I miss you.

She held the dish full of chicken divan and prepared to head up the steps to meet her newest neighbors. Never a social butterfly, Rayna had to force herself to get out, stay in contact with people and avoid spending time with only the animals she photographed. Animals were so much easier to deal with than people. They didn't expect her to hold long, drawn-out conversations or to return their phone calls. They didn't make her empty promises and they didn't leave her alone.

"Can I help you?" The deep, distinctively male, heavily accented voice came from behind her.

Startled, Rayna tossed the dish in the air and narrowly missed dropping it onto the ground. A strong hand gripped her shoulder, and a yelp almost escaped her. Composing herself, Rayna turned and came face-to-face with a tall man with raven hair, a dark goatee and a body deserving of a magazine cover. His silver gaze, while certainly something she'd never seen before, was captivating and put her at ease. "Umm?"

"Umm?" There was no mistaking the mocking tone of his voice. He put a hand in his pocket and glanced at the dish. His nose wrinkled, and for a minute Rayna thought for sure he'd be sick. "What, may I ask, is in there?"

"It's a chicken dish," she blurted out. She'd never been much with conversation starting. "I brought it to welcome you to the neighborhood. I live just down the road a bit. I'm not the greatest cook in the world but I'm not so bad—"

"Chicken?" He gasped, his eyes widening and the blood draining from his face as he reached for the dish, only to yank his hands away, a look of disgust in his eyes. "You brought us chicken? To eat? A bird? For food? For us? I know certain species of birds eat others here, but where we are from that is simply not done."

Puzzled, Rayna took a step back and tried to understand what the problem could be. Had she sold her grandmother's house to a nutjob? What was he babbling about birds eating birds? His accent did make it difficult for her to fully understand him, so there was a chance she'd simply misunderstood. "Are you a vegetarian?"

"A veg-ee-terrian?" he asked, over pronouncing the word.

"Someone who doesn't eat meat," she returned, understanding there was a language barrier between them. "Where are you from?"

"Nowhere you have heard of," he returned, his brows meeting. "You have people who do not eat meat?"

"Yes."

"Are you one?" he asked.

"No."

He glanced at the dish in her hands. "And you eat birds?"

She blushed. "I do."

He cringed.

"Sachin, how much longer must we endure this gods-forsaken realm? And why must we be—"

The silver-eyed man before her seized hold of the dish and stood at attention as if royalty was about to appear. He cleared his throat, his gaze flickering to Rayna for a brief moment. "Kabril, good of you to join us. I was just greeting our neighbor."

"Rayna," she said, eyeing the manner in which Sachin held the dish. He looked as if he thought it would bite him. Unnerved, she glanced over her shoulder to find an equally tall man with the same jet-black hair. She didn't think it was possible to improve upon Sachin's good looks. She was wrong.

Really wrong.

The newcomer was sexy with a capital *S*. This one had eyes of gold, reflecting the midafternoon sun back at her. He also lacked a goatee, though he had the start of a five o'clock shadow. Both men were good-looking to the extreme but this one, there was something about him that made her gut clench at the sight of him. His muscular form was recognizable to her. Flashes from her dreams returned to her and she felt her face heating, as thoughts of carnal pleasures raced over her. Her knees felt weak and her pulse sped as she stared at the man. His gaze raked over her, slow at first, like she was being judged, before it turned into something else. As if he wanted to devour her, and she certainly wanted to be gobbled up by him.

"Kabril." Sachin took a step closer to her, still holding the dish she'd made at an odd angle, as if it were an explosive rather than dinner. "Kabril," he said, this time more forceful than before.

The man closest to her with the golden gaze didn't seem to hear the other as he stared at her. She gulped, her gaze sliding over him more. The lightweight, white shirt he wore was unbuttoned a bit, revealing his tawny, hairless chest—a chest that made her think of her dream and the man in it.

Moisture pooled at the apex of her thighs. She'd never been this turned on by nothing more than the sight of a man. This man was something indeed.

"Kabril!" Sachin shouted.

Kabril nodded, his gaze matching hers, moving over hers as she was doing to him. His sleeves were cuffed to mid-arm, showing off just how muscular he was. If she didn't pull herself together and fast, she'd likely melt into a puddle of desire. She licked her lower lip, desperately trying to push thoughts of tasting his skin from her mind. For a split second, Rayna could have sworn she heard Sachin address Kabril as *my lord,* but she was too swept up in the man's presence to pay much heed to how he was being addressed.

He shook his head, seemingly as caught up with meeting her as she was him. "W-what?" he snapped.

Sachin let out a low chuckle. "Kabril, this is our neighbor Rayna."

"Rayna." Kabril's accent matched Sachin's, neither of which Rayna could place. They seemed European, yet she could not put her finger on where, exactly. He clenched his hands, causing the muscles in his arms to flex.

She moaned and instantly wanted it back.

Kabril's golden gaze flashed to Sachin and his brow lifted inquisitively. "Tell me she is the one."

The one?

Sachin shifted awkwardly and smiled. "The one who brought us dinner? Why, yes. She is. I shall take this inside now. Thank you."

Rayna reached for the dish. "No. I mean, it's okay. You don't have to pretend to want it. I get you're not a fan of chicken. Sorry about that. I just wanted to welcome you and your—" She glanced at Kabril. "—friend to the neighborhood. And, well, I sort of wanted to meet the people who now live in what used to be my grandmother's home."

Sachin held firm to the dish. "There are quite a few personal items still here. Photographs and the like. Kabril and I have put them all in the downstairs extra room. We thought someone might wish to keep them, as they are no doubt of value."

Rayna teared up. She'd thought she could sell the house as it was and not look back. She was wrong. She nodded, thankful they'd been so considerate. Most wouldn't have been. "Yes. Thank you."

Kabril moved closer to her, his hand finding her forearm. Heat raced between them and she swayed. He pulled her closer to his powerful frame. "You are sad."

She swallowed hard. "I'm sorry. I didn't want to get emotional today. I wanted today to be perfect. I thought I could bring you a dish, welcome you, and in the process close this chapter of my life."

"You are who is with the older woman in the photographs within?" he asked. "You have grown. This is good. Very good."

She nearly laughed at his phrasing of things. "Uh, thanks?"

Sachin shook his head. "I truly cannot take him anywhere."

She smiled through her tears. "Oh, I don't know. He managed to lighten the mood."

Kabril tightened his grip on her arm. "You will remain here?"

"Kabril, let the nice young woman go and we can get back to what we were doing."

"Jobs those beneath us do," he said.

Sachin used his free hand to rub the bridge of his nose. "I see we should have arrived sooner so you would have had more time to be less like yourself."

Kabril cast a look over his shoulder.

CHAPTER SIX

Rayna eased closer to the newcomer. "Welcome." A pregnant pause followed and Rayna found herself wanting to fill it. "What brings the two of you to Mississippi?"

She really hoped they weren't a couple. The best ones always seemed to be gay.

Sachin grinned. "We are here to open a new practice for Dr. Kabril Kingston. He's a vet who specializes in wildlife—avian variety to be exact. I'm *just* his assistant."

Did he know that she'd been wondering if they were a couple?

He winked.

She jumped closer to Kabril, making Sachin laugh. She thought more upon what Sachin had said. Kabril was a vet?

Her eyes lit as the knowledge of what the men did washed over her. "You work with birds? I photograph wildlife for a living. Birds are my favorite. I love them. They're so majestic and beautiful." She put distance between she and Kabril, realizing just how close she'd gotten to him.

"I am aware of what you do," Sachin said so softly she almost missed it.

Strange.

Kabril closed the distance between them, his walk that of a refined gentleman but with a tinge of roughness. "I choose this one. She is most pleasing to the eye and…" His gaze slid lower. "…will birth fine sons. She will make a perfect queen."

"Huh?" While it wasn't the most intelligent response she'd ever had, it seemed fitting at the moment. Never in her life had a man said something like that to her and she'd heard some crazy come-ons. The more she thought about his statement the funnier it became. Laughter bubbled up from her as she put her hand out to greet him. "Ah, a jokester. Anyway, nice to meet you, Dr. Kingston. I'm sure you get this a lot, but if you have a chance, I'd love for you to stop by my place and have a look at Henry."

"Henry?" he asked, a jealous note evident. "Who is Henry?"

"Well, maybe Henrietta. I'm not sure if the red-tailed hawk is a boy or a girl. I just know he hurt his wing. He won't let me near him to check how badly, but he seems okay with the idea of me putting food close by." A knot formed in her stomach as she thought about the bird. "Please don't ask me to go into detail on how I feed him. I called a friend of mine who owns a pet store. He drops off mice for me to put out."

Sachin snickered, seeming entirely too amused with the situation. "You care for an injured hawk?"

She nodded.

Sachin looked to Kabril. "I believe you can stand down. 'Tis merely a hawk."

"Those are the worst kind," Kabril said, a teasing note to his voice. Kabril pulled her closer. It was past the point of invading one another's personal space, yet Rayna welcomed it. "I shall see to your Henry and then we will leave this gods-forsaken—"

"Kabril," Sachin said with a warning.

"I have selected," Kabril said, as if it summed up everything. "Remaining is foolish when I have picked what I want. Her."

Sachin tapped his fingers on the dish. "Yes, but the choice is not yours to make, Kabril."

A defeated look passed over Kabril's handsome face. "You mean she is not the one."

29

"Not the one what?" Rayna glanced back and forth between the men. Whatever inside information they were sharing with nothing more than odd looks wasn't something they were letting her in on. "Where are you two from? I'm only asking because I have a sneaky suspicion something might not be translating well. As it stands, it sounds like this one—" She pointed to Kabril. "—wants to snatch me up and take me away."

She should have been opposed to the idea. Anyone in their right mind would be. She was anything but.

Kabril nodded. "Good plan. Come, we shall leave at once."

Rayna laughed harder. These two were too much and she'd been seriously in need of humor in her life. She couldn't remember the last time she'd smiled and meant it.

"No. It is a terrible plan," said Sachin, shaking his head and pointing a finger at Kabril, much like a mother would when scolding a child. "The worst you have ever had and I am old enough to remember when you thought it wise for us to sneak across the river when we were but children to try to see the young maids from the village as they bathed in the cool water. That ended with the two of us having to select which switch we most wanted to be scolded with. Your father took great pleasure in our pain on that day. My arse still recalls as much." Sachin shook his head before going into the house, taking the chicken dish with him, though he held it out far from his body the entire way. He yelled something about wooing but Rayna didn't catch it all.

Kabril grunted and then put his arm out to her, smiling. There was a warmth in his eyes, one that told her there was more to the man than he presented. "Rayna, I would very much like to see to Henry's condition. I can do so now if it pleases you."

She grinned. "Not until you tell me about this village of yours and you wanting to see bathing ladies."

Kabril blushed. "That was a long, long time ago."

"Not that long ago. You're what? Thirty at best?"

He flashed a white, wide smile. "Where is this Henry of yours?"

A man who didn't want to talk about his age or himself much, for that matter, was oddly refreshing. Though, she wasn't sure why he seemed reluctant to speak about his age. He looked incredibly fit and young.

She touched his arm. "He's on the other side of the property, near my home."

"You live close?" he asked.

"I do," she said. "My property line butts up against yours. I'd wanted to be close to my grandmother."

"You were close in terms of family, yes?" he asked.

"Very. She was the only family I had left." She didn't want to dwell on the bad. "What about you? Do you have a big or small family?"

"Large," he said. "Very large." He motioned with his arm, clearly unwilling to take no for an answer. "Lead me to your Henry."

She slid her arm into his. The action was very unlike her but she couldn't deny how good touching him felt. There was certainly something about the man that made her trust him. Her instincts were good, having never led her astray before, so Rayna didn't hesitate to go with them. "Thank you."

"The pleasure is all mine, I assure you." The confident smile Kabril cast in her direction warmed her through to her toes. The man had to be aware of just how good looking he was. "Tell me more of your Henry."

"My Henry?" she mused. "I like the sound of that. Although, I don't own him. He's a free spirit. A wild, beautiful creature I want nothing more than to see back in good health."

"I sense the truth in your words," he said. "You are not like many here. They seek to try to tame all that is wild by nature and they wish to posses it for themselves."

The comment was odd, but from the small bit she knew of him, so was he. "You mean people who have pets?"

31

He said nothing.

"I had a dog once. It was a rescue. Someone had shot out his eye and he only had three legs. I found him on the side of the road and my grandmother and I took him and cared for him until he passed some ten years later."

"This dog was born to be cared for by humans. Some creatures are not."

She thought more about what he was saying. She'd always hated the collectors who kept exotic animals. "I agree. I bet you see a lot of that in your profession."

"I see more of it here than I wish," he said, his jaw tightening.

"You mean the US?"

He took a moment before speaking, seeming to thinking hard upon his words. "It is a problem that plagues this world. Very few of your kind take to heart that they are merely visitors upon this earth, that they should care for it and leave it clean and well cared for, along with its animals."

"You're an environmentalist. I have a lot of respect for those who dedicate their lives to trying to make a difference. I photographed the extreme effects the depletion of the rainforests is having on wildlife there. It's gut-wrenching."

He nodded, his other hand moving to hers as they walked arm in arm as if they had known one another for a lifetime. He didn't feel like a stranger. There was a connection with him she couldn't quite understand, but it was there.

She kicked a loose stone on the side of the one-lane road as they walked towards the place she now called home.

"So, you make photographs," he said, making her laugh softly.

"I take them, yes."

He seemed confused by her statement and again she wondered where he was from. "And you do this with animals?"

"I do. I love them."

"Have you a man?" he asked bluntly.

She missed a step but was thankfully still arm in arm with him so she didn't fall. "Um, no. No man."

"Good. I would have challenged him for your hand."

Challenged him?

She gulped and would have commented but Kabril tugged gently on her arm and used his free hand to point towards the sky. "Look there. Do you see it?"

She looked up and spotted a large bird in the air. The late spring breeze tickled her skin but she ignored the cold as she realized what she was staring up at. "Is that another red-tail hawk?"

"Yes." He drew her closer to him. Heat seemed to radiate from his powerful body and she sank against him, warming herself and enjoying the feel of his firm body. "I believe your Henry is truly a Henry."

Shocked, she shook her head and continued keeping her gaze skyward. "No. That can't be him. He was hurt. I saw him trying to fly but failing."

Kabril chuckled. "That is a female flying above. She's calling for the male. It involves a courtship of sorts."

"So," she grinned, "Henry has a chick?"

"A chick? As in a fledgling?" The serious tone of his voice made her laugh.

"I mean as in a hot woman. A girl. A sexy significant other. A wife. A ball and chain. A…"

As Kabril slid his hand over hers, she stopped spouting off and enjoyed his touch. His golden gaze fixed on her. "A ball and chain? Is that really a description one uses for their mate here?"

"Uh, mate?" Rayna steered him to the side of her house. "Funny, I think your term is stranger than mine."

CHAPTER SEVEN

Kabril drew in the human female's sweet scent. She smelled of roses and sandalwood. Two scents he was familiar with from his visits to Earth and two scents he enjoyed greatly. His loins burned with the need to find solace in her divine body. Her dark hair was pulled into some sort of a twist, leaving long strands of it free and cascading over her slender shoulders. She stared up at him through eyes so blue they nearly stole his breath. When Sachin had told him of the beautiful women to be found on Earth, he'd dismissed him. As he pulled Rayna closer to him, he knew he owed his old friend an apology. Not only was she beautiful, she sparked a primal urge in Kabril that no wench had prior.

Do not call your woman a wench.

Sachin's voice filled his head as if he were part of Kabril's thought process. Perhaps he was, for Kabril could not think clearly on his own around Rayna. She was unlike any creature he had ever met before and he fully planned on whisking her away to his realm the moment she showed any sign of being of a like mind. He was not one for patience or this wooing Sachin spoke of. He much preferred to simply take what he wanted and he wanted Rayna.

The trews, or jeans as Sachin had referred to them, dug at his erection painfully. Kabril believed they should be taken back to his realm and used to torture prisoners. Surely any man wearing them would tell all to simply be free from them. They were too restricting. Or perhaps human males were not as well endowed as his kind. He did not know nor did he care.

He wanted to be home, in his realm, in his clothing—discarded of course—bedding Rayna until she cried his name out in ecstasy. And he wanted to sire sons upon her. Countless sons. They would be brave as he was and perhaps have her smile, for they were not permitted to have her kind heart. One day they must lead and leaders had to rule with their heads, not their hearts.

He smiled as the thought of taking her, pleasing her every way imaginable, left his blood pumping. Sachin's words of wisdom beat in his head. He couldn't steal her away to his realm. Well, he could, but according to Sachin doing such a thing would leave a human female clipping his wings while he slept or unmanning him.

Neither was an option.

Perhaps I could chain her until she submits?

The idea had merit. He could kiss his way down her womanly form to her sex while her hands were bound above her head. She would squirm and he would grant no mercy until he licked his fill of her.

"Do you see him?" Rayna asked, jerking Kabril from his erotic thoughts momentarily.

It was hard to keep from glancing at her wrists, imagining them bound above her head as he licked his way down her body. He had little doubt he could have her moaning in delight before the sun went down. His prowess with women was legendary and she would fall easily into his bed, as all women did.

Her long legs would effortlessly wrap about his body, holding him to her as he pumped in and out. He could almost feel her wet entrance wrapped around his shaft. Kabril swallowed hard, his eyelids fluttering and his breathing erratic.

"Hello, Dr. Kingston?"

He jerked, his gaze darting to her lush breasts. "What? Oh, yes. Please call me Kabril."

She pointed to an oversized tree and winked. "Henry's up there. He's not currently perched on my chest, so if you wouldn't mind, please stop staring at it."

Clearing his throat, he tried and failed to keep a blush from staining his cheeks. He was a king. Kings were not embarrassed to be caught admiring a glorious pair of breasts. And, oh, what a pair they were. He forced his gaze towards the bird, caught slightly off-guard by his randy behavior. "You must be Henry."

I can heal you, little bird. Do not fear me. He pushed with his mind to the hawk currently staring down at him. *Is that agreeable to you?*

The bird nodded in agreement and flapped its good wing. Rayna drew in a deep breath and clutched his arm, her nearness causing his cock to respond more. "Kabril, look. It's like he understands."

"Yes," he said, savoring her tender touch. He wanted her beneath him sooner rather than later. It would be the only way he could continue to fit in the jeans Sachin insisted he wear.

The smile that lit her face moved him, making him think less about bedding her and more about simply pleasing her for the sake of making her smile again. "Do you mind if I grab my camera? I'd love to have pictures of you treating Henry."

It was best she be away while he first worked with the bird, since his ways would differ greatly from those of the human animal doctors. Besides, having Rayna away from him, even for just a bit, might help to alleviate his rock-hard cock. His dick twitched at the thought of sinking into Rayna's body and he knew clearing his mind of her was hopeless. "I would not mind in the least."

She was off and running in the other direction, toward the home that was near. He had to force his gaze away from her and onto Henry.

"Come," he said to the hawk.

It obeyed and did its best to fly to him, its wing clearly injured. Kabril held his arm out, allowing the bird to land upon his forearm. The bird nuzzled to Kabril, lowering its head more, giving heed to the fact Kabril was the dominant of the two of them.

"You wish to fly with your mate again, yes?"

The hawk nuzzled closer. Kabril double-checked to be sure Rayna was out of view from his workings before he did what humans would not understand—he drew upon his magik.

As king of the hawks he possessed more than most shifter males. His magik came to him as easily as drawing in air. It felt good to use it again. He had not dared to tap into his gifts since arrival in Earth's realm for fear he would jeopardize what the Oracle had laid out for him.

For he wanted a mate.

Just as Henry wished to be with his, Kabril wanted someone to bond with. Someone to call his own.

Rayna.

He pushed his magik through Henry, mindful to only use a small amount. He took the hawk's pain but did not fully mend the wing just yet. He would not be able to explain away such a task to Rayna and he knew as much. Sachin would also caution him about using his powers.

Henry settled comfortably upon Kabril's arm and Rayna appeared, her face aghast. She pointed to him while holding a device of some sorts. "You're holding Henry without a glove. Your arm will be torn up."

Kabril merely glanced at his unharmed arm and then back to Rayna. "I will be fine. What is it you have there?"

"My camera," she said, holding it up to her face. She pulled it down and removed something from the front, pink staining her cheeks. "Erm, lens cap was still on."

He grinned, liking being around her more than he should.

"Can you hold him out just a bit more?" she asked, motioning to Henry.

Kabril did as instructed. He would do whatever she wished, for as long as she wished. And he could not recall a time he had ever thought such a thing about anyone. This woman was very different indeed.

CHAPTER EIGHT

Kabril entered the home and found Sachin standing there, arms crossed. His head advisor snorted. "I half expected you to come with the woman tossed over your shoulder, ready to fly home with her."

"I considered it," Kabril said honestly. And he had. More than a few times during their period together. She had taken many pictures, as she called them, though he had no proof of these photographs she spoke of. Humans and their toys often left him in a state of confusion.

Henry played along nicely, doing his best to look more injured than he currently was. The hawk understood Kabril's plight.

"The female?" asked Sachin.

"I walked her to her door as you told me was the custom here when courting a woman. I also did as you instructed on being the human way—I attempted to kiss her while on her doorstep."

"And?" Sachin prompted.

Kabril rubbed his cheek. "It did not go as planned."

Sachin bit his lips and Kabril entertained covering the distance between them and ending his friend. "I see, my lord. Do you wish to spar? The night is young and we do not want you to become a lazy king, do we?"

"Oh, we most certainly will spar." Kabril was itching to get his hands on his sword once more.

Sachin left the room and returned with their swords. He smiled widely. "I thought this might do the trick."

Kabril eyed him. "Why did she reject my advances? Women do not do such a thing to me."

"You are used to women who know who you are and what you are," Sachin reminded. "Rayna does not. Nor, do I believe, she would care in that regard. To her you are simply a man. Not a king."

"I dislike being a man. I prefer wenches to simply come and obey when instructed to," he snapped. The harem was always ready and willing to fulfill any of his needs. He did not have to woo it or court it or whatever it was Sachin took to calling the ridiculous ways in which human males apparently had to conduct themselves with the females.

Why every man didn't have a harem of his own was beyond him. They were quite handy. Though, the thought of returning home to bed one of those women caused something close to panic to well within him.

Leave Rayna?

For another woman?

He could not.

He cursed the gods under his breath once more. Disliking the current state of things greatly. Nothing seemed easy anymore.

Sachin offered a knowing smile. "I understand, but, Kabril, walk carefully with her. She is…"

Kabril held up a hand, dismissing Sachin. "I know. I know. She is not the one. It matters not to me. I select her. The Oracle can shove its prophecy up its backside. I have decided who I want as my queen."

Sachin's lips twitched. "Have you now?"

"I have."

Folding his arms over his chest, Sachin watched him with a pensive look. "And the female's thoughts on this?"

"I have not mentioned to her. I will when the time is right."

"Ah," mused Sachin. "When might that be? Before or after she attempts to feed us chicken again?"

Kabril's stomach turned. "She will not be required to cook once she is queen. I will insist she not."

40

Sachin laughed, deep and loud. "Thank you, my lord. I fear the kitchen staff at the castle is not quite up to cooking other birds."

Kabril glanced back at the door. "When may I see her again?"

"You are asking my thoughts on the matter?" Sachin appeared taken aback.

Kabril groaned. So far this evening he'd been slapped by a woman who held his interest and found himself having to seek counsel from a man he wanted to run through with his own sword. "I am."

"Go to her at first light. Use the injured bird as a reason to see her, but just happen to take along with you freshly picked flowers. Tell her you are sorry for being so forward with her. That the kiss was merely a result of the instant attraction you felt for her and that you do not intend to do it again."

"But I do intend to do it again," returned Kabril, thoroughly confused.

Sachin snorted. "I know that, as do you, but for now, do not say such things to her. She requires time and courtship."

Kabril could not stop the grin from forming upon his face. "This is wooing?"

"It is," said Sachin.

"I enjoy this feeling. Well, when not being slapped."

Sachin flashed a wide smile. "I suspected you might."

CHAPTER NINE

Rayna opened her front door, surprised to see Kabril at such an early hour. When they'd said their goodbyes, the night before, he'd tried to kiss her. What shocked her more wasn't the attempted kiss, it was her knee-jerk reaction.

She'd hauled off and slapped the crap out of him.

She'd regretted it instantly and wasn't even sure why she'd done it. It wasn't as though she didn't want his lips on hers. Still, she'd done the unthinkable.

She'd hit the sexiest guy she'd ever seen all because he'd clearly been attracted to her too. If her grandmother were still alive she'd never have let Rayna live this down. Her grandmother had quite the sense of humor and never seemed to have issues with the opposite sex. Rayna lacked both qualities.

"Fair morning," Kabril said as he stood there, wearing a light-colored shirt, undone even more than the last she'd seen him in, and a pair of tan dress pants. He had a handful of weeds in his hands and the biggest, most handsome smile she'd ever seen a man wear.

"And to you," she returned, still watching him.

He cleared his throat. "My apologies for being too forward with you last night."

She blushed. "Kabril, I'm sorry I hit you."

His brows met. "You are?"

"I am."

"These are for you," he said, thrusting the weeds at her. They were quite possibly the ugliest grouping of weeds she had ever seen.

She held her laughter. He was trying, but it was evident wherever he was from things simply were not done in the same way they were here. "Thank you. How thoughtful."

He nodded as if she were correct—they were *incredibly* thoughtful. Rayna failed to hide her laughter and snickered slightly. Kabril looked her over and then licked his lower lip.

"You are wearing a very thin shift," he said, his throat appearing tight.

She tipped her head, thinking about what he'd said. A shift? Did he mean nightgown? She stepped back, holding open the door. "Come in and I'll grab a robe. Sorry. It's not even five in the morning yet. I wasn't expecting company."

"You were resting?" he asked, sorrow in his voice.

She didn't have the heart to tell him yes. It was awfully early and normal people would be asleep, not accepting handfuls of weeds. "Nope. Awake but not quite dressed for the day."

"I have come to check in on Henry."

Her heart twisted into a jumbled mess of hormones. She loved hearing that he cared for the bird. And her ovaries seemed overly interested in the man. She even glanced down the length of herself, silently scolding them in hopes they'd get a grip before they overrode her mouth and led her to say something stupid.

The man's hair was down again today and she wondered if he ever wore it tied back. It was long enough. Normally, long hair wasn't something she liked on men. On him, it worked.

More than worked.

She half hoped he'd try to kiss her again. She was ready for it this time and she wouldn't allow herself to slap him. No. She'd grab the man, knock him to the ground and attempt a baby-making session because he had that effect on her ovaries.

Pull it together.

43

"I'll change and we can check on Henry together," she said.

He looked around her kitchen area and then back to her. "You enjoy domestic kitchen work?"

Was he asking if she liked to cook?

"Yes," she said, hoping she got it right. "I cook a lot, but it's only me here to eat it so it does take some of the fun out of it."

"And you cook birds?" he asked.

She laughed. "And other things. What about you? Do you enjoy cooking?"

"No," he practically shouted. Then he paused. "Well, I do not believe I would enjoy such a thing."

"Wait. Are you telling me you've never cooked anything?" That couldn't be. He was around thirty. How could he have made it that long in life and never cooked anything before?

He nodded and then looked up sheepishly at her. "Is this a weakness to you?"

"Not at all." Rayna liked the man even more. He needed her. He just didn't quite know it yet. "Then by all means let's check on Henry and then, if you have time, you can help me make something for breakfast."

"You wish to break our fast?" he asked.

A hushed laugh fell from her. Kabril had such odd ways of phrasing things.

"Yes. Something like that."

"Very well," he said. "Because you wish it so."

She paused.

He cleared his throat again. "Rayna, I would very much like to gain your trust and to court you."

She blinked. "Court me?"

"Woo you?"

She nearly doubled over in laughter. Was he for real?

The serious look on his face made her wonder. She put a hand out to him. "Come in and I'll get dressed. We can check on Henry and then we take things slow. Does that work?"

"It does," he said, his hand engulfing hers.

The man was huge and all she could think about was what it would be like to have him above her.

CHAPTER TEN

Earth, one month later…

Rayna walked carefully along the narrow path. The waterfalls around her continued to draw her attention and it was only a matter of time before she either killed herself trying to see their beauty or got the picture she desperately wanted. Hopefully, the second of the scenarios prevailed.

She couldn't believe just how breathtaking the scenery was. Or that Kabril had insisted she accompany him and Sachin on their trip. He was researching something or other and when he'd all but insisted she come too, she knew she couldn't resist him.

The last four weeks had been filled with more handfuls of weeds, lots of long walks, seeing Henry fully recovered, and a good deal of time in the kitchen—as she tried but failed to teach Kabril to cook.

They'd not kissed. It was as if Kabril was taking her request to go slow to the extreme, and the buildup was killing her. If the man didn't kiss her soon she'd likely tie him to a tree and have her way with him.

Her boot slid on the loose gravel and Rayna lost her footing. Her heart felt as if it leapt to her throat and blocked the scream wanting to come. A strong hand caught hold of her, plucking her from the air with an ease and strength normal men didn't seem to possess. As she stared into a set of unnaturally golden eyes, she couldn't help but smile. A nervous giggle sounded from her and her cheeks heated out of embarrassment. Why was she always such a klutz around the man?

He brought out the worst in her as far as being able to walk without falling on her face. Maybe if she spent less time staring at his body and more time paying attention to what she was doing, she wouldn't appear to have two left feet.

"Careful, I would very much like you to remain in one piece," Kabril said, his voice so deep and so sexy that Rayna had to bite back a sigh. She still had yet to place his accent. It wasn't thick but it did tinge his voice ever so. She'd often tried to get exactly where he was from out of him, but Kabril liked his secrets and she didn't mind letting him have them.

He set her on her feet and visually inspected her. "Are you hurt?"

"Just my pride." She tipped a bit, losing her balance, and seized hold of his forearm. The man didn't seem to have an ounce of fat on him. She squeezed and visions of having Kabril's powerful body above her, sliding in and out of her, filled Rayna's head. Sex with him was pretty much all she thought about. What woman wouldn't?

She couldn't tear her gaze from his square face and piercing eyes.

He glanced over the edge. "I am dangerously close to making you wear a safety harness, Rayna. You, unfortunately," he puffed out a long breath, "do not have wings."

"There is a better than average chance I'd wring my neck with the harness so it's best you not." It was true. She seemed to be all thumbs around him. She'd even managed to set her toaster on fire with him in her kitchen. The man was probably questioning her ability to cook, let alone teach him.

Laughing, he held her close to him. "I have no doubt you would. You are so very different from most women I know."

"Hey, is that a knock on how clumsy I am?" She grinned, enjoying his teasing more than she should. His warm hands seemed to push heat through her body as he held her close. Rayna shifted awkwardly in an attempt to stop the moisture Kabril was more than capable of producing between her legs. One glance from him and Rayna's body reacted.

"No. Not clumsy. More like absentminded," he whispered, the bass in his voice moving over her, causing her to sigh. "But I would change nothing about you. Though, you having wings could be something indeed."

"Mmm, wings. That would be weird but cool." She drew a deep breath in, savoring a mix of lavender, sage and cedar—the scent of Kabril. She stroked his chest, his shirt in the way of her getting to paradise.

He dipped his head. "Be mindful of your footing. I beg of you," he said, his lips close to hers. "I want you safe."

"Thank you for bringing me on this trip," she said, still caressing his chest.

He remained in place. "I would never dream of leaving you behind."

"Kabril?" she asked, her voice shaky.

"Yes?"

There was so much she wanted to ask. None of that came out. Instead, she boldly went to her tiptoes and pressed her lips to his. The last time they'd had anything close to a kiss she'd slapped him. She wasn't sure if he'd push her away or not.

Growling, he lifted her off her feet, his mouth claiming her in a hot, possessive manner. His tongue darted into her mouth and she moaned, her mind a jumbled mess of desire.

There were far too many articles of clothing between them. She wanted this man naked and ready, but she'd take him anyway she could get him. She bunched his shirt, theirs lips still locked, her heart pounding madly in her chest.

The man could kiss unbelievably well. And she'd had the nerve to hit him when he'd first tried it. Had she known it would be this good, she would have insisted they do this much sooner.

"Rayna, you dropped this," Sachin said, coming up from behind, causing her to jerk away from Kabril.

Kabril released her and she touched her swollen lower lip, her pulse still racing and her hormones raging. Fierce desire shone in Kabril's eyes and she feared he might actually yank her back to him and finish what he'd started. While she wanted that desperately, she did not want an audience.

Sachin held a lens cap to her camera in one hand and had a rather large smile upon his handsome face. He looked between the two of them and paused. "Am I interrupting something?"

"Yes," said Kabril. "Go away."

"No," Rayna interjected, reaching for the lens cap. She couldn't believe she'd dropped it. "You're fine. Thank you."

Sachin grinned. "You are most welcome."

"Go away," repeated Kabril.

Rayna shot him a hard look. "Stop it."

"No," he said with a pout. "You permitted me the pleasures of your lips and did not slap my face. He needs to leave. At once. I wish to sample more of you."

She turned several shades of red.

Sachin grunted. "Kabril."

Kabril looked to Sachin for what felt like forever to Rayna before he sighed. "Very well. I shall wait and continue to woo her."

She giggled and both men's attention moved to her. "Come on. Admit it, he's funny."

"Oh yes, he is known for witty ways," Sachin added.

Kabril growled.

She touched his hand and looked around the area. "It's so beautiful here."

"Yes, you are."

"Hmm?"

He glanced over the edge of the drop. "Yes. It is lovely."

"Is it wrong that I don't ever want to go home?" she asked.

Sachin snorted. "But then how will you finish teaching Kabril to make toast?"

"If I kick him in the shin, would it hurt things between us?" she asked of Kabril. She knew the two were very close, maybe even related, but Kabril tended to avoid talking much about how long they'd known each other or if they were blood.

"Should you do such a thing, I would find you even more endearing and more than likely whisk you away from here and keep you all for myself."

She nearly melted at his words. She eyed Sachin's leg.

Sachin backed up. "No abusing me. Kabril does it enough for the two of you."

"And you goad him every chance you get," she reminded.

He shrugged. "It is what I do."

She held her lens cap to her. "I swear, around you, Kabril, I have two left feet and I'd forget my head if it wasn't attached."

He paled. "Your head can detach?"

She laughed and pushed past him, mindful of the steep ledge. "Are we going back to camp or are you two going to start exchanging weird looks when you don't think I'm watching you?"

No sooner did the words come out her mouth than Kabril and Sachin did exactly that. They glanced at one another. Sachin's expression was one of amusement. Kabril's held something else. Something Rayna couldn't pinpoint. It was too cute not to comment.

"See, that's exactly what you do to me. You always make me feel like I'm missing out on an inside joke. It makes me crazy." Lunging forward, she ruffled Kabril's chin-length black hair. His smile warmed her heart. "There. That's more like it. I hate it when you look like the weight of the world is on your shoulders. You brought me because you wanted to do a photo journal, documenting your studies. As much as I'm loving this vacation, I like to see you happy more."

Kabril caught her hand and drew it to his lips, planting a kiss on the back of her hand tenderly. Before Rayna could remark, Kabril had drawn her into his arms. A slow, racy smile moved over his face. She wanted another kiss, but not in front of Sachin. Not with the way Kabril kissed. The man was nearly X-rated.

She swallowed hard. Her pussy responded with a spasm and she had to focus on something, anything other than Kabril or risk begging him to fuck her against the rocky wall. "We should get back to camp. It'll be getting dark soon and I still want to take a bath."

Kabril perked up. "A bath?" He exchanged another long look with Sachin and nodded. "By all means, camp it is then."

"You are so weird," she said, laughing softly as she fell in line behind him. Rayna's gaze landed upon his luscious ass and she closed her eyes. If gawking at the waterfalls didn't get her killed, Kabril's tight butt just might.

"Be careful of your step," said Kabril as he slowed his pace, falling behind. She knew he wanted to speak with Sachin without her listening in.

CHAPTER ELEVEN

Kabril waited until Rayna was far enough in front of him before turning to Sachin. His heart was at war with his head. He'd seen Rayna nearly fall from the cliff's edge and all he could think was that his woman was mortal and had nearly suffered a fate he could not bring her back from. All his shifter instincts screamed at him to take her and fly away home to his kingdom with her. That the human realm wasn't safe enough for her.

She belonged with him.

The only problem with his plan was that he'd spent the last month lying to her—keeping his true identity and the fact he was a bird shifter from her. She thought him nothing more than a human male.

"Thinking upon the kiss?" asked Sachin. "It is progress… the 'her-no-longer-slapping-you' bit."

Kabril's voice shook as he spoke, "She would have died had she fallen."

"She would have to be able to move more than ten feet from you to be in any real danger," Sachin chimed in, sarcasm lacing his every word. "You do not let her out of your sight, my lord. Seems unlikely she would be in any real danger."

It was true. Kabril did not let Rayna out of his sight.

"Had I not been there…"

Sachin touched his shoulder. "You were there, Kabril. She is safe and well."

Kabril looked in Rayna's direction Rayna. "She makes me feel things I do not recall ever feeling before."

Sachin seemed pleased. "We best catch up with her for fear she fall from the path—again."

Gasping, Kabril shot forward, tapping into his shifter speed as he rushed to Rayna, Sachin's laughter following him all the way.

CHAPTER TWELVE

Kabril stood quietly, watching from the shadows as Rayna bathed by the river's edge, silently wishing she were his chosen one—his mate. She was the one he longed for. The one he thought about birthing his sons. Not some nameless, faceless woman the Oracle spoke of. Kabril held no feelings for whoever the prophecy mentioned. His feelings were for Rayna and Rayna alone. He liked that she was what she referred to as clumsy and that she enjoyed cooking, even if she did cook birds. He liked that she loved animals of all sorts, shapes and sizes but that she was especially drawn to birds.

You more than like her, he reminded himself. *You love her.*

He sighed. He did not want whatever woman the Oracle thought best for him. He wanted Rayna. And he would have her. He was king. He would simply make it law that she was to be his queen.

He'd fallen behind in his duties as king but didn't want to be separated from Rayna just yet. Sachin's original plan had been to bring Kabril to the human realm for a week or two, introduce him to his chosen mate and then get him back to his duties.

That had not happened. Rossi was overseeing things back home and Kabril was confidant in his brother's ability to rule—even though Rossi was young and tended to enjoy drink and women over actual work. In addition, stirring had started about the *Falco Peregrinus*. They wanted more power and more land. To gain both they would need to go through Kabril's kingdom and overtake it. He would not allow such a thing to happen. Rossi would handle affairs for now but if war broke out, Kabril would have no choice but to return home.

Kabril had obligations to his people. Already he had planned not to carry out on the prophecy they all held so dearly. The least he could do was be there to rule himself. Not leave his brother to serve in his place.

But going home without Rayna was simply not an option. He ached for her day and night. He thought of her at all hours. And the kiss had only reaffirmed his obsession with her. His cock was hard now as he watched her off in the distance, bathing in the fresh water. It was wrong to watch her without her knowledge.

Sachin had pointed out as much but Kabril did not care.

Claim her.

He understood his ways were barbaric in comparison to what Rayna was used to, yet he could not stop the overwhelming urge to rush to her, sink his cock into her and say the words that would bind them for all eternity. She would be his then. Prophecy be damned. He was king. He could do as he pleased. He did not need to answer to anyone.

Perhaps if I take her home, the prophecy will assume one human female is as good as the next?

No. It would never work and he knew it. Still, it didn't hurt to dream.

A pang of guilt swept over him as he continued to watch Rayna bathing without her knowledge, but he had rationalized it out several nights after arriving at the campsite. All of his kind possessed varying degrees of magiks. It was no surprise one of Kabril's strongest gifts was that of being able to control other animals. After all, he was a leader by birth. The jungle wasn't exactly safe to wander about alone. Bathing in the river was even less safe. So long as he was near, he could mentally will the other animals away from his mate.

My mate. If only that were true. I would happily accept the human before me.

The words played about in his head. Never had he thought they would sound so perfect. Then again, he hadn't planned on finding Rayna. He'd expected something else and would no doubt get it whenever he found the mate Sachin swore was close. He'd get something other than the beautiful, loving woman before him. Rayna was divine. Everything he wanted in a wife and so very much more. Within the first week of meeting her, he'd all but forgotten she wasn't like him. Wasn't a *Buteos Regalis*. It didn't matter. Nothing but claiming her and making her his wife did.

If only I could.

His loins burned with the need to possess her. Thoughts of bedding Rayna plagued his dreams and remained a constant in his waking hours. The woman's scent alone was enough to drive a man insane.

Roses and sandalwood.

Even now Kabril could still smell her lingering scent on him. His cock dug painfully at its confines and he swallowed hard, hoping his erection would go down on its own. Seeing her naked wasn't helping matters.

Rayna wore her long hair pulled into a loose bun at the top of her head, as she always did when she bathed late at night. His preternatural eyes could see perfectly in any light. The tiniest of freckles graced her nose and tanned shoulders whenever she'd been in the sun too long. The caramel look the sun's rays left her with was intoxicating. Kabril wanted to lick every inch of her, see if she tasted as delicious as she looked.

She will taste even more divine.

Glancing over her shoulder, Rayna stared in his direction. Kabril knew the darkened shadows covered him and didn't bother to move. He let his gaze rake over her slowly, taking in the sight of her breasts. Her nipples were dark and puckered as if waiting for him to take them into his mouth. Reaching down, he undid his pants and slipped his hand in, fisting his rigid cock. He needed release or he'd risk the beast side of him taking over and possibly claiming Rayna—not bothering to wait for

56

this mate Sachin swore he was close to finding. A mate he did not want for he only wanted Rayna.

Kabril seriously considered simply plucking Rayna from Earth, taking her to his home and demanding she submit to him. Sachin was right. The ways of old would not work with an Earth woman. Especially not one as headstrong as Rayna. No, she would have removed vital parts of his anatomy. Though, dying by her hand would be acceptable.

He stroked his cock, staring at the small swell of her lower abdomen and imagining his tongue there, licking, tracing its way to the juncture of her thighs. Kabril knew Rayna had only a small thatch of well-maintained hair upon her mound because he spent many a night assuming the form of an Earth-sized hawk and watching her. It was not exactly comfortable to take on the form of a creature so much smaller than his normal shifted form, but he did it all the same. At six-foot-six in human form, Kabril was even bigger shifted, quite a difference from the size of an Earth hawk. Also a significant difference between Rayna and himself in normal form.

Rayna seemed so tiny to him, so petite, that at times he worried if he would harm her should he sink his cock into her and claim her for all time. Sachin assured him all would be well when the time came, should his actual mate prove to be Rayna's size, but Kabril couldn't think past her. *She* was who he wanted in his bed, swelling with his sons and ruling by his side for all eternity. Thoughts of hurting her didn't sit well with him. Since Sachin had a tendency to wander from Accipitridae to Earth when he assumed Kabril wasn't paying attention, and bed human women, Kabril trusted his judgment on the matter.

Kabril watched her closely as he continued to stroke his cock. Every muscle in his body was tight, hungry for Rayna. Her gaze remained locked on his area. Could she see him?

No.

That was foolish.

She was but human and lacked the extraordinary vision of the shifter races. Still, her gaze remained. As he ran his hand down the length of his shaft, Rayna touched her stomach, the same place he'd envisioned licking. As her fingers trailed their way to the apex of her thighs, Kabril's breathing grew shallow. Would she touch herself as well? Better yet, would she think of him while doing it?

That's it, ta'konima—*my love. Touch yourself. Show me how you wish me to touch you.*

Rayna cupped a breast with one hand and let the other hand slide between her legs to the place Kabril desired to be. As she parted her slit, he had to fight off his orgasm. He should last longer than he did while masturbating. It was almost embarrassing how quickly even the thought of Rayna could make him lose control. Holding the base of his cock firmly, Kabril managed to narrowly avoid spilling his seed. The sight of Rayna fingering herself, rubbing her clit while she stared in his direction was too much. He palmed himself and stroked as fast and as furious as he wanted to take her. He wanted to pummel his cock into her silken depths until both their bodies were spent and his seed planted in her.

Rayna rocked against her hand, riding it to the point it glistened with her cream. The scent of her arousal permeated the air, filling Kabril not only with lust but with the carnal knowledge that he would take her and soon. It was no longer a choice. Between his obsession with her and the news coming from Accipitridae of the *Falco Peregrinus'* repeated attempts to take power, Kabril had to return for good—and soon. Leaving without his mate wasn't an option.

She's not my mate, he reminded himself. *But if I have any input in my affairs, she will be my queen.*

It mattered not what the people thought of him should he return home without his destined bride. All that mattered was that he could not survive without Rayna in his life.

He loved her and he could not recall loving anything in his very long life.

Rayna shook her hips slightly as she arched her neck. From the tiny whimpers to the way her body twitched, he knew she was coming. Stroking his cock faster, he didn't fight it when his body wanted release. Instead, he came with her, sending come jetting from his body into the brush before him, all the while keeping his gaze locked firmly on Rayna as pleasure ripped through her body.

Something rustled across from him, on the other side of Rayna, and Kabril fought with his still erect cock to get it back into the confines of his pants. Rayna apparently heard the noise as well, which was strange considering how faint it was. She dressed quickly, pulling on her shirt and slipping into her shorts. The knowledge she wore no undergarments would consume him the remainder of the night. Visions of her coming by her own hand would grip him for centuries.

CHAPTER THIRTEEN

Rayna glanced in the opposite direction of camp and did her best to focus in the darkness. If it weren't for the light of the moon, it would have been pitch black. The jungle had been eerily silent while she bathed, right up until she'd given in to the urge to touch herself. Spending her days and her nights near Kabril was proving to be too much for her. Back home, she could at least get away from the lure of him because he had his practice and she had work. Since he was a veterinarian and her passion was photographing animals, it seemed fitting they spend time together. She'd spent months in various remote corners of the Earth, chasing down that perfect picture of whatever animal it was she'd been sent to shoot.

After being charged by two very angry tigers, Rayna had decided to avoid anything bigger than her for a while. In fact, it was Kabril's idea she take some time from her normal work and aid him with his research. He'd even tried to pay her much more than she'd ever dream of charging. Rayna wouldn't hear of taking his money. While she wasn't rich, she was comfortable.

Looking around at the beauty of the tropics, Rayna knew she'd made the right decision in coming on the trip. The environment was soothing and she couldn't imagine being away from Kabril for the month he had planned to be away. That, more than anything, had prompted her to accept his invitation. She'd grown accustomed to seeing him daily, hearing his laugh and simply knowing he was close.

She even enjoyed time with Sachin. His odd sense of humor complimented Kabril's, making him a welcome addition. He also seemed to watch over Kabril. It was out of the ordinary but Rayna never questioned it.

The sound of a twig snapping and leaves rustling grabbed Rayna's attention. Nothing seemed off, yet her inner alarms were going off. She squinted in hopes it would help her see whatever was there. Thoughts of jaguars and other jungle predators filled her head, making her jerk back as fear crept over her.

She stepped onto the shore and dressed as quickly as she could. Her shorts clung to her wet body as did her shirt. As Rayna bent down to grab her boots something splashed in the water. No part of her wanted to dwell on what wildlife called the river home. Still, the urge to glance over at the water bordered on overwhelming. It appeared still and what little moonlight made its way through the canopy of trees managed to reflect off the water's surface.

Something splashed again, this time sounding much closer than the last. The hair on the back of her neck stood on end and the urge to flee was great. Never one to back down from a challenge, Rayna hesitated, sure her mind was playing tricks on her. Taking a deep, calming breath, she nodded.

It's probably a frog or something.

Rayna turned to head back to camp and ran face first into what felt like a truck. A really warm, muscular, fantastic-smelling truck.

"Ouch."

"Rayna?" Kabril asked, the sound of his voice making her feel safe.

Relief swept through her and she tossed her arms around his neck. He stood tall, taking her with him. She dangled for a moment and went to release him. Kabril didn't allow it. He wrapped his large arms around her and held her off the ground.

His golden gaze locked on her. "Rayna?"

Her mind wanted her to tell him she was fine and to put her down. Her body had something altogether different planned. She swallowed hard and did her best to pull herself together before she did something stupid, like beg him to fuck her.

"Umm, Kabril," she whispered, running her hand through the back of his hair. "You're going to hurt yourself. Put me down."

"You are naught but chest high and scarce weigh more than a feather," he said, his speech suddenly sounding so very different than normal. Thoughts of castles, knights and men of power filled her head.

Rayna rolled her eyes playfully and snorted. "The 'I could have fallen out of the pages of a medieval romance novel' vibe you got going is cute. Put me down now." She pushed lightly on his upper chest but Kabril didn't release her. "Please…my lord."

"No," he said quickly, still holding her. "To you, I am always Kabril."

Confused but willing to play along, Rayna nodded. "So you're saying I can't give you cute lil' pet names like pookie bear and honey bunches?"

"Bear?" He licked his lower lip and she had to fight back the moan that wanted to come. "Not the animal I hoped for, but if you wish. Though, I might take to calling you *mine*."

The idea of belonging to him left Rayna shivering in anticipation. She could only imagine what it would be like to have Kabril sliding in and out of her body, taking and giving pleasure until they could no longer move. Her erect nipples poked through the wet material of her shirt as she wiggled to get down. They scraped against his muscular chest and pleasure shot through her, leaving Rayna hissing as if she'd been burned. Kabril slid a hand lower and cupped her ass. Her breath hitched as heat flared through her body.

His warm breath skated over her cheek and he chuckled. "Something wrong?"

"Yes...erm...no." She bit her inner cheek, trying and failing to rid herself of the heat he caused. "I think I'm on fire."

Kabril dragged her against him, causing her to rub along him just right. "On fire?" he asked, sounding all too keen on hearing more.

Denial was futile. She nodded and Kabril lifted her chin, forcing her to face him. Capturing her mouth with his, Kabril left her legs quivering and her holding tight to him for fear she'd fall during his sensual assault. Rayna fed from the sweetness of Kabril's mouth. The kiss was intoxicating, as she knew it would be.

Kabril dominated their kiss, circling his tongue around hers and leading every step of the way. "Rayna," he murmured, continuing his glorious invasion. He held her cheek with one hand and her body with the other. The sheer power in his arms was not lost on her.

"Kabril," she said breathlessly. "Please."

Please put me down was what she was going to say. It wasn't what came out. Good thing, considering being put down was the last thing she truly wanted to have happen. He slid his hand under her wet shirt and Rayna didn't stop him. Instead, she ate at his mouth, kissing him with the hunger of a crazed woman. For a month she'd longed to have him do this to her and wasn't about to stop it now. She didn't have the willpower to make him stop, even if she wanted to.

The next thing she knew, she had her legs wrapped around his waist and her arms around his neck as he worked his hands further under her shirt. He tweaked her nipples, rolling them between his forefingers and his thumbs with a precision she didn't want to question. The idea of him bedding other women sickened her.

"Rayna," he murmured, kissing her neck and cupping her breasts. He nipped playfully at her shoulders and let out a manly chuckle as she rubbed against him.

Rayna wanted more. She needed to feel him inside her. There were too many articles of clothing between them. She tugged at his open shirt, running her hands over the planes of his chest. His muscles rippled under the weight of her touch and Rayna lost the ability to control her breathing. She shifted her hips, rubbing her body against his, stroking his long, thick cock just right. Release was near. She arched in wild response, pushing her clit against his clothed erection. His lips greeted hers at the same moment her orgasm struck. Kabril drank her moans down, smothering them with his kisses. She wanted more.

Kabril jerked his hands out from under her shirt and she unwrapped her legs from his waist. He eased her to the bank and she squirmed beneath him. This was what she wanted. He shoved up her shirt more, his head dipping, his mouth covering her exposed nipple.

Moaning, Rayna arched to him, her hands in his hair as he tasted from her body. This was just as she'd dreamed—the same way her dream lover had handled her.

As she ran her hands over Kabril's back, forcing his shirt up as well, she realized he was exactly like the man she'd dreamed of.

It's him.

Kabril leaned up long enough to remove his shirt and cast it aside and then he was back, his mouth on hers before she could think anymore on the knowledge she'd dreamed of this man. His hands were suddenly on the top of her drawstring pants. He made quick work of them and she was thankful, at least for the moment, he was a skilled lover. She wasn't sure she had the patience for anything but.

At least not when it came to him.

He eased her pants from her and went to his knees, gazing down at her—her shirt pushed up over her breasts, her pants gone. She felt vulnerable and too exposed. As she made an attempt to cover herself, Kabril caught her wrists.

"No," he said sternly. "I wish to look upon you. You are stunning."

He lowered himself and ran his hands over her body. Each swipe of his fingers left fire racing straight to the apex of her thighs. Dammit. She wouldn't last like this.

"Kabril."

He grinned and it was devilish, promising pleasure if she could wait.

She couldn't.

She pouted, her lips pursing as she made another move to touch him. Shaking his head, he sent his long hair flying about his face as he seized both her wrists with one hand.

He held her there as he traced his other hand between her breasts. "I enjoy looking at you."

She batted her eyes, her breath coming out in pants.

"I watch you," he said in a deep, powerful voice. "I watched you bathe on this night."

She tipped her head. He had? The idea turned her on more. "Have you watched me other times?"

"Yes," he said, running his hand to the juncture of her thighs. Her wetness greeted him and she moaned as he slipped his finger closer to her entrance. "On many occasions."

She understood this was behavior she should frown upon, but the idea he'd wanted her in such a way only turned her on more. She'd have watched him too if given the chance. She smiled up at him and reached down, her hand moving over his.

She was so close to getting pleasure from him when he stopped, sat up fast and retrieved her pants. He handed them to her. "Cover yourself. Sachin nears."

"What?"

His breathing was off. "Rayna, unless you wish me to take you like a savage on the edge of this river for any to see, cover yourself."

Nodding, she did as instructed, a little tempted to say screw it and let anyone who wanted to watch, enjoy the show. After all, she'd wanted this man since she'd met him and it was high time they did the deed instead of dancing around one another. Had she moved quicker with him, she'd already know what it was like to have him in her. She could only imagine it would be sheer perfection. Just like Kabril.

She dressed as quickly as she could, considering she was still damp from the river and everything in her ached for sex. Kabril whimpered as she tied the drawstring to her pants.

"I very much want to be with you," he said. "I want us joined as one."

"I want that too," she replied, unabashed. He did that to her. He made her feel wanton and wild. And she loved every second of it.

CHAPTER FOURTEEN

"Kabril?" Sachin appeared from the shadows, silencing any further confessions that might have fallen from her lips. His silver eyes were narrow and he seemed focused on something behind them.

Rayna was a tad surprised Sachin didn't comment on the fact she was being held off the ground by Kabril. He seemed fixated on something else. Her brow furrowed. "Sachin, what's wrong?"

His gaze met Kabril's. "We are not alone."

Kabril tightened his hold on her to the point she could scarcely draw in air. "K-a-b-r-i-l."

He released her quickly, causing her to stumble. Sachin was there in an instant, steadying her. Kabril growled and gave her a slight tug, pulling her away from Sachin. The men stared at one another for what felt like eternity. Testosterone coated the air. Scared of a possible wild animal stalking them, Rayna batted them both on the arm. They were acting like idiots, so she didn't mind stooping to scolding them. "Guys? What happened to *we are not alone*? Huh? I don't want to be the main course for a jaguar. Pull it together here."

No sooner did the words leave her lips than tension seemed to fill the air. Suddenly, the sounds of the jungle all but halted. Her breath hitched and she took a small step towards Kabril. As silly as it sounded, he made her feel safe regardless what she might have to face.

"How many?" He glanced towards Sachin.

Sachin's gaze never left the surrounding area. He shook his head slightly. "I do not know. Take Rayna to safety. I shall see to—"

Kabril scoffed. "We are in unfamiliar territory, old friend. I will not leave you to your own devices. Not when it is clear we are outnumbered."

"Your first concern is Rayna," said Sachin. "I am aware of as much."

"Yes, but if we do not eliminate the threat then…"

Rayna stared at Kabril, noting his speech was different once again, as was Sachin's. "Guys?"

"Worry not, *ta'konima*," Kabril whispered, putting his body before hers. He kissed her tenderly. "All will be well."

She arched a brow, wondering what the hell it was he'd just called her. From the sound of Sachin's sharp intake of breath, she had a funny feeling it meant something significant. Her luck, he'd just insulted her in the worst way and she was oblivious.

He crouched a bit, taking her with him. Sachin followed suit. Kabril motioned with his head towards the far left of the river. "They are coming in from that way as well."

Sachin nodded, appearing to have already caught on to the fact they were being surrounded. Rayna was still lost. "Wait? Jaguars are now hunting us in a pack? I thought they weren't ones to travel in groups. I thought—"

Her words were cut short by the sudden sound of something swooshing overhead. Kabril tossed his body over hers, taking her down and pressing her to the ground. He shouted something to Sachin, but the noise level reached proportions that drowned him out. Besides, she didn't think it was English.

As quickly as Kabril's weight had landed on her, it was ripped off. Rayna sat up fast, pushing to her feet. The sound that could only be described as hundreds of birds flapping their wings ended. The strangest part of it all was that Sachin and Kabril were missing, leaving her alone on the edge of the river.

"Kabril?" She turned in a slow circle, doing her best to pierce the darkness with nothing more than her eyes. It was a blackness like she'd never experienced before and she'd spent her fair share of time outside of big cities. Still, this was different. Eerie even. She felt threatened, though she wasn't sure exactly what was doing the threatening. The men with her weren't really big on sharing, and at the moment she desperately wanted them each back by her, even if it meant being stared at funnily by them. "Sachin?"

Fear gripped her.

"Kab-ril?" she asked, her voice cracking under the weight of her nerves. "This isn't funny. You two have the strangest sense of humor. Kabril?"

Nothing.

Rayna wasn't sure how much time passed but she knew it was a significant amount. Something rustled in the brush to her left and she froze. "Kabril?"

A single feather drifted down before her face, nearly causing her to scream. Calming herself, Rayna plucked it from the air. The bird it belonged to had to be huge. The feather was over a foot long and had something dark, warm and wet on it. She brought it closer to her face and gasped when she realized it was blood.

She turned quickly and ran head first into something. Strong arms grabbed her shoulders and she gave in to the urge to scream a half a second before she brought her knee up, hard and fast.

"Rayna." Kabril deflected her knee with his upper thigh right before she would have made contact with his groin.

Her eyes widened as she realized it was him. "What? Where? Kabril?"

A soft smile slid over his handsome face, easing some of the tension in her body. "I am here and you are safe."

"What about Sachin?"

"Here," Sachin said, appearing behind her, causing her to push her body against Kabril's.

Rayna pressed her forehead to Kabril's chest. "You two need to hum or something when you walk. You scared the hell out of me. And where did you go? You just vanished."

"We saw to the threat," he said gently. He ran his hand through her hair and then kissed her lips. "I am sorry you were frightened. I assure you, we would allow no harm to come to you."

She glanced around. "Are the jaguars still close? I think they attacked a bird." She held the bloody feather up for Kabril to see. "Poor thing."

His gaze hardened. "Discard that immediately, Rayna."

Stunned by the directness in his voice, Rayna simply stared at him. She'd never seen this side of him and wasn't sure she liked it. "Kabril?"

He ripped the feather from her hand and tossed it aside. "Return to camp this instant."

She blinked, sure she'd heard him wrong. He couldn't be issuing orders to her like he was her master. "Excuse me?"

He pointed towards the campsite. "Go!"

Sachin moved up next to her and cleared his throat. "Kabril."

"What if the bird's not dead, Kabril?" she asked, deciding to seize the moment. "Shouldn't we look for it? You could help it. It's what you do, right?"

"Cease your chatter, woman." Kabril's nostrils flared and his entire body went rigid. "I gave you an order. Do not disobey me on this."

Rayna took a giant step back. He suddenly seemed like a stranger before her. An arrogant asshole of a stranger. Anger consumed her, leaving her throat constricted as she fought to keep from crying out with rage. Something on Kabril's face changed as a sigh tore free of him. He made a move to come to her but she put her hand up, stopping him. "Don't. I'll do what you *command*. I'll go back to camp, but know that I'm doing it to keep from choking you, not because you ordered me to."

"Rayna, no." Kabril made another move to come to her, this time finding Sachin stepping in his path. "I did not mean to—"

She folded her arms over her chest and gave him a droll look. "Didn't mean to what? Open mouth, insert foot? I'm sorry I asked about the bird. I assumed since you're a vet and all that you'd care. Guess I was wrong." She glared at him. "About a lot of things."

Sachin glanced over his shoulder at her. "Rayna, forgive him. The, umm, jaguars—" He nudged Kabril. "—yes, jaguars, left him worried about how safe you were. He is not acting like himself right now. He worries about you. We both do."

"Yet you don't bark orders at me like I'm a dog." She gave Kabril a cross look. He cringed under the weight of her stare. "Don't you think I was worried about you two? Huh? For all I knew, you two were being mauled to death twenty feet from me."

Kabril lowered his head.

She pointed at him. "Jerk. Here I thought you were different from other men. You're just the same, aren't you?" Rayna didn't wait for an answer. Instead, she turned to head back to camp, mumbling on the way, "Cease my chatter? Thinks he's king of the jungle. Asshole."

CHAPTER FIFTEEN

Kabril winced at the sound of Rayna cursing him as she headed towards camp. She had every right to be upset with him. He had reacted poorly to the idea that the enemy's mark was near her. The feather, that was just a feather to her, was so much more to him. It was a part of the enemy. An enemy that had come too close to her as was. Kabril would not allow threats directed at him to leak onto her.

And his temper could not be settled at the moment. He knew as much. She would be safer far from him. The falcons would want nothing to do with a human. They would not dirty their hands with the likes of her. That was good. If they were focused on him, she would be safe.

He had never been more thankful that his kind—the bird shifters—thought of humans as pests. In this instance, it would save Rayna's life. He twisted, his gaze wild as he looked to Sachin. "I killed at least two. You?"

"Two as well," returned Sachin. "But there were more, Kabril."

"Go with Rayna. I will lead them far from here."

Sachin sighed. "I cannot and will not leave you. Though, I do not think you should have sent her off alone."

Kabril's chest tightened with worry. "Keeping her near me placed a target upon her. Now she is merely a human female. They will have no use of her."

Sachin appeared nervous. "Still, my lord. Perhaps we should keep her close."

"So that my enemies can see that she matters to me?" he demanded, pacing, his shifter side wanting free. He flexed his arms, wanting to release his wings, track the bastards who had dared to attack them and remove their heads from their shoulders. How dare they think to threaten him with Rayna near? Did they not realize he would kill any who even looked in her way with thoughts of aggression on their minds?

He stopped pacing and met Sachin's gaze. "Take her and protect her."

"Kabril."

"Then track the others and I will take her to safety!"

"I will not leave you or her. We should go to her now." Sachin wasn't acting like himself. Something was wrong. Kabril spoke, "They will not want her, correct? She is but human. They will have no interest in her, right?"

Ah, there was a point I too thought I would never have an interest in a human either. Now look. I am at the mercy of one.

"She will hold value to them, my lord, because she holds value to you," Sachin said, his words cutting Kabril like a knife.

He was right.

He tried to go in the direction of camp but Sachin stopped him. "I will go. She is none too pleased with you at the moment. I cannot blame her. You were what the humans like to call a dickhead." Sachin coughed slightly and shook.

It took Kabril a second to realize he was being laughed at—again. He punched out quickly, catching Sachin's right cheek. "I do not find this amusing. I hold her in high regard."

"Do you?" Sachin mocked. "I would have never guessed. I mean, with all the nights you have spent in shifted form, doing your best to reduce your size to that of an earth bird—the shame in that alone is enough to suggest you more than hold her in high regard, but you are not ready to admit the true extent of your feelings for her. Are you?"

He scowled. "I wish to know how the enemy found us? The falcons know I am here therefore they know Rossi is sitting on the throne in my absence."

"Your brother will protect the kingdom," stated Sachin. "Your place is here and now."

"Yes, the prophecy you speak so much of." Kabril spat to the side. "I curse it and all it stands for."

Sachin looked tired. "Again?"

"Yes, again."

"Forgive me if I hide my shock. Now, as for Rayna."

His chest tightened at the thought of Rayna falling into the enemy's hands. He couldn't believe his enemy had tracked him down on Earth and attacked. "She is most displeased with me."

Rubbing his jaw, Sachin nodded. "I know. You did not have to take your anger out on Rayna. She was unaware the feather belonged to the Falco. Her heart is big. Her concern for you is even bigger. Did you not sense the fear in her voice when she called your name?"

Kabril had sensed her fear. It had eaten at him as he flew high in the air above her, killing the enemy and disposing of them downriver. It had pained Kabril greatly, not being able to shout out, let Rayna know he was near. The last thing he wanted to do was have her find out what he truly was during a battle. She wouldn't understand.

Sachin patted Kabril's shoulder. "Go. Fly for a bit and clear your mind. I shall guard Rayna."

CHAPTER SIXTEEN

Still muttering curses, Rayna headed for her tent. She couldn't believe how arrogant Kabril was suddenly being. Sure, he tended to say odd things and come off as old-fashioned but he'd taken it too far.

Way too far.

She had half a mind to go back and kick him square in the backside. How dare he speak to her like that? Especially after they'd finally taken the next step. They'd made out. If he didn't have a way of making her body feel like she'd fallen through the gates of heaven she might actually find him and drown him.

The idea had merit.

"Men are jerks," she mumbled. She was about to continue on her one-woman tantrum when something shuffled to her side. Glancing in that direction, Rayna froze as she spotted a man she didn't know standing there, a wild look about him. He had very long, very blond hair that was partially tied back with leather straps. That wasn't the weirdest part. The guy was wearing a loincloth.

Nothing but a friggin scrap of material over his groin. She had to be hallucinating. No one ran around in a loincloth.

Did they?

She swallowed hard. The way he was glaring at her through eyes of burnt umber said he wasn't there to ask for directions to the nearest village or chitchat.

No.

He was up to no good. Her mind tried to rationalize why he was there and where he'd come from but she came up empty. They were in such a remote area of the jungle that no one should have happened upon them.

She thought back to the odd behavior from Kabril and Sachin—when she'd assumed jaguars were stalking them. She realized then that neither man had really said as much.

"So you are the human their king is so fond of," he said, his voice deep. He had the same hard to place accent as Kabril and Sachin. Fear rushed over her.

Rayna took a tiny step back, already understanding the man meant to do her harm.

A wry grin spread over the stranger's face. "Running is pointless. Come quietly and I shall make your death as painless as possible."

My death?

She yelped.

The man moved closer, walking in a wide circle around her. Everything about him screamed predator yet she got the sense he was actually struggling with himself. As if hurting her might go against his nature.

Great.

Crazy jungle serial killer with a conscience.

Rayna lifted her hands as if to say, no threat here. Which there wasn't but still. She felt the gesture might be needed to prove she wasn't anything the man should worry about. Other than the fact she wanted to scream until she went hoarse. Maybe Kabril and Sachin would hear her and come running.

Or maybe they wouldn't.

Maybe she was totally on her own.

She'd never believed herself to be a fighter. She'd also never had her life in jeopardy such as now. Something deep within Rayna snapped. She bent down quickly, seized hold of one of the retaining wall rocks for the fire and pitched it at him. A scream tore free of her as she did. The man sidestepped the rock with ease, looking amused by her efforts to keep him at bay. The dirt she'd accidentally cast with the rock rained down upon him. His laughter faded instantly as some of the dirt made its way into the wound on his side.

He lunged at her. Rayna tucked and rolled away from the fire pit, kicking with one leg as he approached. She scored a direct gut hit. Pain radiated up her leg. The man was solid muscle. He snaked an arm around her waist and the next thing she knew, she was being lifted off the ground.

High off the ground.

What the hell?

As the campsite below seemed to shrink, her stomach dropped and fear held her screams. She knew she should call out. Do something. Anything to alert Kabril and Sachin of what was happening, but she could scarcely wrap her mind around it, let alone warn others.

CHAPTER SEVENTEEN

"Calm down," Sachin said, keeping a safe distance from Kabril.

"Calm down?" he echoed, wanting to kill something, anything. "The woman I wish to rule by my side for all eternity runs off into the jungle rather than spend another moment with me and you tell me to calm down?"

"We will find her, my lord."

Kabril froze. "Why is it you are not correcting me—telling me how we will find my mate soon and that Rayna can never rule by my side?"

Sachin whistled as he averted his gaze. A sinking feeling came over Kabril as he clenched his fists. He knew Sachin well enough to know his old friend was up to his antics again. "Why is it I think you have been trifling with me from the moment we came to Earth?"

"Perhaps—" Sachin kept his gaze directed anywhere but at Kabril. "—it is because I have been trifling with you."

"What?" he bellowed.

Sachin stiffened. "I know you, Kabril. You would have resisted your pull to her had you known the truth. It is part of your stubborn nature, *my lord.*"

"The truth?" Kabril arched a brow in question, not liking the added my lord. "What truth?"

Sachin held his secrets close. Growling, Kabril stared at his long-time friend. "This conversation is far from over. Now we hunt for Rayna. Once I have her safely within my sight, you will tell me all you have been keeping from me."

"As you wish, my lord." Sachin bent his head and yanked his shirt off, shifting into partial hawk form as he did. Large brown and white feathers rippled over his shoulders as a set of wings emerged from his upper back. Sachin, like Kabril and most other strong warriors, could shift portions of his body on command without pain and for indefinite periods of time. They could also do full shifts if need be.

Kabril did the same, shifting enough to be able to fly. As his wings sprouted forth from his shoulder blades, Kabril took a deep breath, enjoying the rare treat. While on Earth, he had to use caution not to be discovered. Shifting was a luxury. He flexed his wings, each spanning close to ten feet, and took one last look around the campsite.

He shouldn't care that Rayna walked out on him, but he couldn't help himself. Even if she wasn't the woman the prophecy spoke of, he'd come to care for her. The jungle was no place to wander alone. Especially not with an enemy attack having just been thwarted. As Kabril went to lift off the ground, he noticed something near the doused fire pit. One of the retaining wall rocks was missing.

He glanced around the area and found it off to the side of the site. There was something else there. A single bloodied feather. Not the one he'd forced Rayna to drop—a new one.

Suddenly, it felt as if he'd been struck in the midriff. The air swooshed from his lungs and his knees weakened. He was unable to believe they'd missed a Falco warrior, even with the proof lying right before him. Kabril clawed at the ground, shaking his head in denial as his body contorted in pain—partially shifting, then un-shifting, at an alarming rate. Vaguely, he heard someone crying out. It took a moment for him to register the fact that it was him and that he was calling for his mate—his Rayna.

CHAPTER EIGHTEEN

Kabril held tight to one of his advisor's throats. The urge to choke the life from the man was great. "Speak out against my decision again and I will kill you with my bare hands."

Rossi, his brother and soon-to-be the next target of his rage, touched his shoulder tentatively. "Kabril, unhand him. He speaks only the truth. To invade *Falco Peregrinus* with no preparation, to rescue, what—a human female who is not even your chosen one—is beyond foolish. It is deadly."

Swinging his fist, Kabril caught his brother's jaw and sent him hurtling into the thick castle wall. "They have *my Rayna*! I am king here. When I order an attack, it is to be carried out. No questions asked."

Rossi stared up, his blue gaze icy. "You have not been king here for many moons."

"Think you to overthrow me, little brother?" Kabril asked, his voice bristling with anger.

"Why should I not?" Rossi was always the one to butt heads with Kabril. Second to the youngest, he was a long way from actually seeing the throne for himself but had the leadership skills needed in Kabril's absence. "You abandon your people on a quest to retrieve the one the Oracle foretold coming, yet you are gone for many moons before returning with tales of another female. You then wish for our men to rush to their deaths to save a pathetic, vile human. Seems to me, big brother, overthrowing is the least I could do for you. The female's life is not worth even one of our own, let alone hundreds upon hundreds."

Sachin stepped forward and delivered a swift kick to Rossi's side. "Speak no ill of your future queen! Rayna is a wonderful, loving human who has done as the Oracle predicted and won the heart of our king."

A chorus of gasps followed Sachin's statement. The advisors began whispering amongst themselves while Kabril stared at his long-time friend. Sachin's words began to sink in and Kabril felt his resolve crumble. He'd not been in his right state of mind from the moment Rayna went missing and suddenly, Sachin's hints hit Kabril with the force of a hundred men. "She is my...my...my true mate?"

Nodding, Sachin lowered his gaze but stood proud. "On the day you first laid eyes upon her, my lord, you whispered how sweet she was and that you would give all to have her be the one. I knew better than to tell you she was your mate because of how stubborn you can be. You did as I'd hoped you would do. You made her like you, won her trust and, I believe, her heart."

"But I lost her." The words fell from his lips in more of a sigh than anything else.

Sachin glanced at the table full of advisors. "Our queen has been taken by our enemy. All of you are aware of the prophecy. Should our lands once more know the sound of children, we must act quickly. Our king wishes to strike with our combined power. Dare you deny him this?"

CHAPTER NINETEEN

Rayna sat, her knees tucked under her chin and her gaze planted firmly on the back of her abductor. The man, or whatever he was, leaned over, dipping his hand into clear water and using it to rinse his wounds. Each time he brought the water to his open flesh, he hissed, leaving Rayna little doubt about how much pain he was in. He'd favored his side for a while. She noticed right away how filthy the wound was, caked in dirt and blood.

She slid her foot back and forth on the river's edge, still unsure where she was. The area, while dense in foliage, trees and flowers, wasn't the same as where she'd been. It also wasn't as humid.

The man glanced over his shoulder. "We are in the Tocallie Mountains. In the Accipitridae realm."

She opened her mouth to comment but he cut her off. "And no, this is not Earth."

Not Earth? Accipitridae realm?

Closing her eyes, Rayna tried and failed to process all that had happened. Men who grew wings and flew in the air didn't exist. Other realms didn't exist. None of this could be real. She pinched her arm, trying to wake herself up, but realized it was a living nightmare.

"W-who are you?"

The man continued to cleanse his wounds. "An enemy of your king."

"My king?" she asked, not following.

A sardonic grin spread over his face. "I suppose you would not view Kabril as your king. Humans have no respect for anyone other than themselves. Not that I advocate showing allegiance to the likes of a *Buteos Regalis*, especially that one in particular, but it is better than answering to no one. Our leader may have his faults, yet we, for the most part, stand behind his decisions." He didn't sound so sure of himself.

Rayna wondered if the man truly believed in what his king did or if he merely wanted her to think he did. Either way, she had no intention of dying by his hands. "Is threatening to kill an unarmed woman considered a fault?"

His gaze lowered slightly as if he were ashamed. He stiffened, suddenly looking composed. "We have more values than the *Buteos Regalis.*"

A Buteos Regalis?

Her mind raced and what she landed on did little in the way of clearing up matters. "Royal hawks?"

The question forming on the man's face alarmed her. One of them needed to have a clear idea of what was going on and it sure as hell wasn't her. "Either you are a skilled liar or you truly do not know."

"Know what?"

"Who and what we are," he said, his voice even.

Suddenly, the idea of knowing everything terrified her more than her current state of ignorance. Blood-tinged water slid down the man's bare torso and into the top of the loincloth he wore. Rayna glanced around, trying to see if anything would work to bind his wounds.

"If your goal is to escape, you should understand the portal back to your world is at an elevation from which you will plummet to your death. Should you attempt to cross it without one of us there to hold you, it will not end in your favor."

"I was looking for something to help stop your bleeding," she said, not bothering to hide her annoyance with the man.

"Oh." He appeared puzzled and then something in his expression seemed to soften. "I am Lazar of the *Falco Peregrinus.*"

She clutched her knees to her chest tighter. "As in a falcon?"

The corners of his mouth twitched slightly. "Yes. As in a falcon. And your name is?"

"Rayna, as in not in Kansas anymore, Rayna," she said, unsure why she gave him any details without fully understanding what was going on.

"I am sorry to be the one to tell you of all you did not know." Lazar went to one knee and looked out from sympathetic eyes. For an abductor, he wasn't as fearsome as he'd first seemed. Setting aside the fact he had wings that sprouted from his upper back and then disappeared within seconds, he wasn't so bad.

She steadied her breathing and avoided making any sudden moves. "Does it hurt?"

Lazar lifted a brow and glanced at his wounds. "I have been hurt worse."

"I meant your wings. When they come out and go back in, does it hurt?"

A slow, steady grin spread over his face. "If I go too long between shifting, my skin itches and I long to feel the air against me as I soar in the skies above. But no, the shift itself is painless."

"Why," Rayna focused on the ground, "did you call Kabril a king? He's a doctor and he doesn't have wings."

The sick feeling in the pit of her stomach returned and she was positive she didn't want to hear Lazar's answer. He cleared his throat and she met his gaze. "How is it you could spend so much time with him, yet know so little?"

I'm wondering the same thing.

She shrugged.

"Maybe you are not the one he seeks. When I witnessed the two of you conducting the starts of coupling, I thought you were she. The human it is said he is destined to mate with."

Rayna ran her hand through the grass next to her, wanting desperately to be home. Her bottom lip trembled as the thought of Kabril taking another woman to his bed beat at her mind. The implication of what Lazar was saying wasn't lost on her. "Kabril is like you? He can—" She ripped a handful of grass from the ground and clutched it to her. "—grow wings too?"

The pity in Lazar's eyes only served to cut deeper into her heart. None of what was happening was a dream. It was as real as the grass she held and the air she breathed. It also meant Kabril had lied to her. Gained her trust and used her.

"My orders were to seize the human female, alive or dead, and return to the castle at once." He looked to the sky. "I do not think it wise to follow these now."

"W-why?"

"Because it is clear his omissions have hurt you enough. I wish not to see my king inflict more pain upon you for simply falling prey to our enemy. As I have said, our king is not without fault. Trust when I say he is not a king anyone sets an innocent before. There is a time to follow blindly. This is not one of them."

Inflict more pain?

Rayna gasped. "They want to hurt me? Why?"

His refusal to answer left Rayna wondering how much to the story there was. Lazar was clearly hiding something. What? She wasn't sure.

Lazar touched his wounds with reluctant fingers and she knew he was in a good deal of pain. "We should rest. Others will come in search of you."

"Others?" Rayna moved towards him quickly, no longer caring that he had the ability to sprout wings.

Lazar chuckled. "I will allow no harm to come to you, Rayna."

She eyed his wounds, the one on his side in particular and snorted. "No offense but I don't think you're—"

"The soil from Earth has something ours lacks. Something in your soil inhibits our ability to heal quickly. Under normal circumstances, my wounds would be nothing more than faint scars by now."

She vividly recalled the dirt hitting him after she threw the rock. "I'm sorry."

Lazar patted her hand. "You were attempting to protect yourself. You have nothing to be sorry for. I—" He sighed. "—on the other hand, do. As soon as I am able, I will return you to your realm. It would be wise if you were to disappear for a while there. The Falco wish greatly to possess you. They believe King Kabril will lay down his sword and barter for your safe return."

Envisioning Kabril wielding a sword wasn't as hard as it should have been. All the times she'd referred to his behavior as regal and his speech as implacable haunted her. As much as she wanted to argue the point that Kabril wasn't the king Lazar spoke of, in her heart she knew Lazar spoke the truth.

She picked a purplish-colored leaf from a plant near her and dipped it into the crystal clear water. "This isn't poisonous, is it?"

Lazar shook his head and chuckled. "No. The flowers the plant will get late in the season are harvested and used in medicine. Was your goal to poison me?"

Rayna knew he was joking. She took the leaf and pressed it to his open wound as gently as she could. He hissed but let her continue, pulling leaves, wetting them and putting them over his open wound.

He caught her hand in his and stared at her, their faces dangerously close. "You tend to me when, by rights, you should be vexed by all I have brought upon you."

"Without you, I'll plummet to my death, remember?" She smiled, trying to make light of a situation she wanted nothing more than to crumble and cry in. Falling to pieces would accomplish nothing. She wanted to go home. Lazar could get her there. Something about him seemed genuine and she needed someone to trust.

86

His smile faded as his gaze flashed towards the sky. "Run!"

Confused by his sudden change, Rayna simply stared at him. "What?"

Dark shadows eclipsed the sun. In an instant Rayna was yanked to her feet by her hair. She cried out and tried to break free, only to find herself being thrust towards a hulk of a man. Dark brown, almost black wings spanned out at least twelve feet in each direction. The menacing stare he leveled on her shook Rayna to the core.

"Humbert," Lazar said, his voice strained. "No."

The brute holding her glowered in the direction Lazar's voice had come from. "Is this the human?" His lip curled. "Disgusting creatures."

"No. I took the wrong one. She was near their king but is…"

Humbert's lecherous gaze slid over her, making her skin crawl before moving back towards Lazar. "You have always been weak where females are concerned." He spat as he glared at Lazar. "The king anticipated as much from you, Lazar. He sent you to test your allegiance."

"But I seized the wrong—"

"It matters not. She will not be permitted to leave now that she's seen our realm. And you, Lazar, you shall be handled accordingly." The man untied one side of his loincloth and fear coursed through her veins.

Lazar moved quickly, attacking the man nearest him. In an instant, the man was sinking in the water, his throat sliced open. Lazar's fingers were bloodied. She looked closer and realized his fingernails were now long, dagger-like. She had little doubt they were the weapon Lazar used to kill the man, even in his weakened state. He held his wounded side and staggered. "Humbert, I will not…will not…"

He swayed and went to one knee, dashing Rayna's hopes of being spared from Humbert. She tried to rush past Humbert but he extended his wings, blocking her path. He stuck his chin out defiantly. "Going somewhere?"

Without thought, Rayna kicked him square between the legs. Humbert doubled over, clutching himself as a choked gasp broke free of him. Her gaze snapped to Lazar. Beads of sweat broke on Lazar's brow and he swayed a bit, touching the ground with one hand to steady himself. Rayna rushed to his side. "Are you okay?"

He nodded a second before his eyes rolled to the back of his head and he tipped forward, splashing into the water. Rayna didn't hesitate. She dove in after him. The icy water shocked her system but she didn't stop. She continued onward, reaching for him through the clear, cold water.

CHAPTER TWENTY

Kabril grabbed hold of his chest and felt as if someone had hit him with a block of ice, stealing his breath. His arms cramped and he lost his focus for just a second, but long enough to jar him from flight. His wings folded in, cradling his body as he fought and failed to draw in air. Something seized him from behind, lifting him and ceasing his decent.

"Kabril!" Sachin's voice pushed through the pain, clearing Kabril's head.

The icy feeling vanished almost as quickly as it had arrived. The innate knowledge something was wrong with his mate settled over him. His iron will surged forth. "Rayna!"

"What vexes you, my lord?" Sachin asked.

"Rayna is hurt. The situation is grave."

"Is she…?" Sachin swallowed thickly. "Is she still alive?"

As much as Kabril wanted to believe she was safe and all would be well, his gut told him differently. He pushed off Sachin and flew in the direction his mate's distress signal had come from. "I do not know."

The Tocallie Mountains spanned a great distance and were easy to get lost in. Nothing could keep him from Rayna now that he'd connected with her on another level. Sachin tried to change course, heading in the logical direction—towards the closest portal—but Kabril remained steady, following the pull of his mate. A clearing appeared and he spotted a Falco warrior near the edge of a spring. Red tinged what should have been crystal clear water. A knot formed in his throat as his heart hammered furiously.

Rayna.

A strangled cry ripped free of him as he began his rapid decent. Kabril broke through the surface of the icy water, already knowing how cold it was. The velocity at which he hit the water left him shooting past his target. Rayna's long hair danced in the water, lifting and swaying with a sickening silence as her limp body headed downwards. A Falco warrior was near her, his body lifeless as well. Kabril recognized him immediately as one of the men he'd fought with. Torn between rage and concern for Rayna, he thrust his anger down and seized hold of his mate. Her body was as cold as the water she was submerged in.

Holding her close, Kabril kicked, using his powerful body to take her quickly to the surface. He drew in a deep breath the moment he emerged, but Rayna did nothing. Her body remained listless. Every fiber of his being called out to the Epopisdeus, begging them for forgiveness and to spare the life of the one he loved.

More than loved.

The scope of his feelings hit him hard. This was his woman. His destiny before him and she was gone. It couldn't be. He'd had only moments with her, what felt like seconds in the span of his long life. He wanted more.

Needed more.

He could not go on if Rayna were not by his side. She had somehow managed to become his everything and so very much more.

"Rayna," he breathed, unshed tears filling his eyes as his chest tightened at the thought of losing her. He could not remember when he had last wept. Kings did not cry. They did not show weakness.

For her I would give up everything.

Someone pried Rayna from his cold hands before someone else yanked him free of the water. Kabril knew his men were close, trying to help, but he needed to be near Rayna.

"N-no!"

His teeth chattered as he reached for his mate. The moment he touched her cheek, a sob fell from his lips. "Magaious, I beg of you, take my life in place of hers. Take me. Spare her. She is young. A long life before her. I have lived many hundreds of years. Me for her!"

He meant every word. He didn't want to walk the path of life without her there. Without her smile, without her laughter.

A circle of gasps sounded around him but Kabril ignored them. It mattered not what his men thought, only that Rayna survived. He would rather die knowing she lived on than to go a single day without her by his side.

CHAPTER TWENTY-ONE

Sachin stood silently watching his long-time friend hold firm to the woman he'd grown to love. It pained Sachin, knowing he'd withheld the truth of who Rayna was from Kabril. He directed his gaze skyward and closed his eyes as Kabril openly prayed to the Epopisdeus he'd shunned so long ago. Sachin joined in, silently calling upon the bird gods to intervene.

He glanced to the side and found Humbert being lifted away, his wings, hands and ankles bound. Curses spat forth from his foul mouth and Sachin vowed to cut the man's tongue from his head before the night was out.

His men lifted a second Falco warrior from the depths of the frigid water, not bothering to tie him. They followed behind Humbert and the others in the direction of the castle. Sachin didn't need to instruct his men to put the two in the dungeon. It went without saying. He did have to give a rather stern look at the remaining guards, fearing they'd take it upon themselves to kill the Falcos instead of allowing the king the pleasure.

Sachin eyed his friend and went to turn his back to give Kabril a private moment for mourning Rayna when a bright light shone down upon them. At first, it bordered on blinding before dimming enough to allow Sachin to make out Kabril's and Rayna's outlines.

The sound of Rayna coughing was music to his ears. It was as if the heavens opened and harps played. Afraid his imagination and wishful thinking had run away with him, Sachin watched his old friend carefully. The moment Kabril tipped his head back and let out a fierce growl of triumph, Sachin drew his sword and held it high.

"Praise Magaious!"

Kabril rocked Rayna, holding her so tight Sachin wondered if his friend would hamper her already labored breathing. He moved to Kabril's side quickly. "I can carry her while you regain your strength, my lord."

Rayna's blue eyes drifted shut and her head lolled back. Kabril kept hold of her. "No."

"Kabril," he whispered, putting his hand on his friend's shoulder. "You are in no condition to fly with her in your arms. You could drop her. Is that what you truly want?"

The weight of the decision showed in Kabril's eyes a second before he handed Rayna to Sachin. The trust given to him was not misplaced. Sachin inclined his head before securing Rayna and taking flight. Kabril flew close to him, no doubt monitoring Sachin's care of his mate.

CHAPTER TWENTY-TWO

Rayna's head felt heavy and her body laden with lead. She groaned as she opened one eye to peer out into the darkened room. Light filtered in through heavy drapery. The single slit and the tiny amount of light passing through left her shielding her face. She tried to roll away but her body refused to respond to her commands.

"Be still," a deep, familiar voice whispered near her ear.

"Kabril?" Rayna asked, twisting around and suffering the fate of such a choice almost instantly. Pain shot through her and she cringed.

Kabril put his hand to her cheek and cupped it gently. "*Ta'konima*, I beg of you to rest. The healer has given you something to help you sleep."

"My arms are heavy and I'm mad at you," she blurted out.

The corners of his lips twitched. "I know. It will pass, as will the pain. I can only hope your anger with me subsides as well, Rayna. If I could take your pain from you, I would. My power does not extend to that point."

Her brow knit as his words trickled through the recesses of her mind. "Power?" She drew in a shallow breath. "Wings? They had wings, Kabril. Huge wings that came right out of their backs. They could fly." She closed her eyes as a dull throb began in her head. "They said you were a king and that you had wings too."

She waited for Kabril to laugh. He didn't. Instead, he simply watched her through cautious golden eyes. Rayna's gaze darted around the room. She'd been in Kabril's bedroom once before, to help him pack for the trip. This was not his room. This room was grand with vaulted ceilings and lamps suspended from chains. The oversized four-poster bed they lay in was carved from dark cherry-colored wood. The Mediterranean blue, plush coverlet engulfed her and matched the silken gown she now wore. Her heated gaze flashed back to him and locked on the tawny expanse of his chest.

Suddenly, her mouth was very dry.

"W-where are we and why are we in bed *together*?"

"Excuse me, my lord," a feminine voice said, causing Rayna to sit up faster than her aching body allowed.

She swayed and Kabril was there, steadying her with his powerful arms. "Rest, Rayna."

Ignoring Kabril, Rayna focused on the female in the doorway. The woman held a tray of what looked to be fruits and a decanter of something. Her long blonde hair fell in waves to her slender waist. As much as Rayna didn't want to be jealous, she was.

The woman inclined her head and offered a non-threatening smile. "My lord," her attention went to Kabril, "Rossi ordered food be sent up. Your brother worries because you have not eaten since..." The woman averted her gaze. "Since...erm..."

"Since the queen arrived?" Kabril supplied, a teasing note in his voice.

Rayna had thought the blonde was gut wrenching enough. Hearing there was a queen to go along with the king left her feeling as if she'd been struck with a bat. "You have a queen?"

"I do," he said, his lips quirking with a half smile.

She touched her stomach lightly, feeling as if she might be ill. She motioned to the blonde. "Who is that?"

Kabril blushed. "She is no one of importance."

The blonde said nothing, she merely kept her head lowered.

Oh, she was someone all right by the way he was acting. She cast a questioning look on him. He squirmed on the bed and cleared his throat. "She, perhaps, was a member of the harem."

"Was a what?" Rayna asked, her head spinning. "Did you just say harem?"

"I did."

"I'm dreaming, aren't I?" she questioned. "This is a nightmare, isn't it?"

Kabril shifted more, his gaze averted.

Rayna's throat tightened. "She's not only part of a harem. She's part of a harem you've been with!"

The woman gasped.

Kabril sat up straight on the bed. "My sweet Rayna, I have disbanded the harem. They are no more. You are the only woman for me. Ask her."

Rayna blinked up at him. "You have got to be kidding me."

"I do not jest," he said, his chest puffing out. "I disbanded the harem upon your arrival here. They no longer service the men of the castle in the same way they once had. This pleases you, yes? Sachin said I should give each of the women within the harem a large sum of money and send them elsewhere."

"I like Sachin more than you at the moment." She looked up and shook her head. "Waking up and finding myself in my boring country house would be great right about now. Really, I'm full up on winged macho men. I'd like to go back to simple, sexy bird doctors. Ones who may be odd at times but don't have stacked blondes showing up to feed them grapes."

"Set the tray down and leave us," Kabril said. "Someone will come with enough money to see to your family's needs for many cycles. Your service is no longer required. I thank you."

The woman did as she was instructed.

Rayna rubbed the back of her neck and let out a soft laugh. "Am I crazy? Be honest."

"Rayna, your sanity is not in question." He ran his fingers down the back of her arm, making a shiver ripple through her. When he reached her hand, Kabril laced his fingers through hers, the move intimate. He brought their joined hands to his lips and planted a chaste kiss on hers. "What I wish to know is if you can accept me as I am."

"You're not a vet, are you?" she asked, already knowing the answer but needing to hear the truth from him.

"To your people, I know more of birds and animals than they could ever hope to." Kabril lifted her hand and spread her fingers wide, kissing the tip of each one. "But, alas, I am not."

"And you're not just foreign, are you?" she asked.

He licked his lower lip. "Yes and no. I am not from your realm. And you are no longer within your realm either. You are now here, in mine."

"Where is here?" She wanted to yell at him for lying to her, but the feel of his full lips trailing over her skin was too distracting.

"Accipitridae. The realm of the bird shifters."

She paused. It was all a lot to soak in. "It was all real?"

"It was." He made his way up her arm, slow and steady. When he reached her shoulder, Kabril nipped lightly at her skin, catching the strap of the gown she wore. He dragged it down before returning to kiss his way up her shoulder, towards her neck.

CHAPTER TWENTY-THREE

Kabril knew Rayna needed her rest, but the taste of her skin was too tempting to resist. He thought she'd shriek in fear of him after he learned she knew he was not human. Once the castle doctors had informed him she would indeed recover, Kabril had set out to learn what had happened from the sources. By the time Kabril reached Humbert, Sachin had already beaten the man within inches of his life. Kabril didn't question Sachin on the matter. If his friend felt the need to take such measures, they were clearly called for.

Lazar was slow to recover and in his fevered state revealed snippets of the conversation he'd held with Rayna. Kabril had wanted to be the one to tell Rayna all his secrets, not have her learn by way of kidnapping at the hands of his enemy. The minute Lazar regained full consciousness he would be tortured for his role in the attack on Rayna. There was little point in inflicting pain on a man who was not aware of the goings-on around him.

Pushing thoughts of torture from his head, Kabril concentrated on the bounty before him. His mate. His soon-to-be wife. Rayna stared at him with questioning eyes and he wanted to kiss the doubt from them. He'd sensed her unease with the serving wench and didn't need to search far inside himself for the reasons behind her mood. She was jealous. It was foolish, considering he'd never given the wench a second look, much less bedded her, but the comfort from knowing Rayna cared if he did left his heart swelling and his lips sealed.

He moved his hand across Rayna and managed to ease her to the bed. Sliding over her, Kabril tried and failed to control his breathing.

Her hair fanned out around her as she stared up at him with wide eyes. His senses were keen and he picked up on the beating of her heart. As much as he wanted to take her, ram his cock into her depths and claim her for his own, Kabril knew she needed to fully recover. "Sleep," he whispered, going to plant a kiss on her forehead.

Rayna tilted her head and caught his lips with hers. She thrust her tongue into his mouth, causing Kabril's chivalry to crumble. His cock hardened at an alarming rate and he rubbed his body against hers. The need to join with her was great. He drew air through his flaring nostrils, behaving more like a rutting bull than the king of hawks. He pressed his distended flesh to Rayna's mound and it only took a second before he felt the proof of her arousal.

"You are wet, *ta'konima*," he whispered between kisses.

Rayna pushed on his chest. "And you are rude. Get off me. Now."

Her spunk only added to her allure. He nodded, making no effort to bend to her wishes. Instead, he feathered his tongue over her bottom lip and relished the shiver that moved through her.

Rayna's foot made its way up the back of his leg before she wrapped her legs around his waist. The feel of her countering his movements was too much. Kabril gave in to the desire to go further. He'd already had a small sampling near the river and could scarcely await more.

He settled between her legs, a reminder that she wore nothing under the sleeping gown he'd had her put in. His own sleeping pants pulled taut as his cock fought for freedom, the promise of paradise close.

Rayna raked her fingernails down his back hard enough to cause his skin to welt but not hard enough to draw blood. The shifter in him could smell even small traces of blood.

She returned his kisses, searching his mouth with her tongue and no doubt finding it welcoming. Rayna arched against him, leaving his cock rubbing against her wet slit. Moisture soaked through his pants and the scent of her arousal pushed him over the edge of restraint.

Growling, Kabril ran a hand into the back of Rayna's hair and tugged, forcing her head back so he could devour her neck—smothering it with heated kisses. He moved downwards and planted kisses on the swell of her breast. Kabril pulled the other strap of her gown, freeing her glorious globes in the process. He took a pink-tipped nipple into his mouth and sucked evenly. Rayna's moans spurred him onward. He squeezed her breasts, cupping them with his hands while he coated them in kisses.

"So sweet. Like ripe berries." He licked a line around her erect nipple, staring up at the rapture on her face.

Her mouth fell open and a cry broke free. "Kabril. Please."

Working his hands down her body, Kabril continued to vary kisses and licks on her nipples. He kneaded her thighs, all the while fighting an internal battle to keep from coming as he inched the gown upwards. He dipped his head, laying kisses low on her stomach. As he neared the thin thatch of well-maintained hair on her mound, Rayna lightly ground her body against him. "Patience, *ta'konima.*"

He spread her drenched folds and eyed the prize. Her rosy clit was swollen with lust. Kabril drew it into his mouth, mindful to be gentle, and flicked his tongue back and forth. Rayna's entire body tightened and he had to seize hold of her hips to keep her from moving up and off the bed.

She cried out, laced her fingers in his hair and held firm, riding his mouth. He lapped cream from her slit while taking one hand and stimulating her clit. He found a steady rhythm and chuckled into her pussy as she began murmuring a mix of curses, pleas and threats.

"Dammit, Kabril. Uh, more. There." She thrust her hips upwards. "There. Oh, yes!"

Rayna came with a start and Kabril continued to work her clit, swirling his tongue and lapping her juices. Her cream was every bit as sweet as she was. Unable to resist her any longer, Kabril moved up and over her. He supported his weight with one arm as he freed his cock from its confines with his other hand.

He nudged her entrance with his cock head and locked gazes with her. "Rayna Vogel, do you accept me—all of me from now until the end of time?"

CHAPTER TWENTY-FOUR

The look Rayna leveled on him was scorching. Purring, she cupped his face and Kabril anxiously awaited her answer. In order for his claim to be official and for Rayna to be the queen in the eyes of his people, she had to accept all of him—his magik included.

A lone tear made its way down her smooth cheek and Kabril felt as if his heart had shattered. Assuming she was rejecting him as her mate, he went to move away. Rayna held steady to his face.

"Kabril?"

"Y-es." He cleared the emotions lodged in this throat. "Yes?"

"Does your skin itch too, when you're not able to shift forms for a long period of time?"

The question caught him off guard. Stunned, he nodded.

She traced a path down his neck and to his shoulders. More tears escaped their watery prison and Kabril had to look away to avoid weeping himself.

"I never meant to cause you pain."

"Rayna?" He wiped her cheek. "What do you mean?"

Her voice shook. "You didn't…change…because of me. Did you?"

Kabril moved slightly, causing the head of his cock to press into her hot core. Fire shot through his lower body and the fierce need to lay claim to what was his was almost debilitating. "Rayna, please. I beg of you. Do you accept me—all of me from now until the end of time?"

She stared up through lust-filled eyes. "Show me, Kabril."

His body felt as if it were going to burst. "Speak not in riddles, *ta'konima*. Though I may be a king, I am still but a man."

The slow, sexy smile that slid over her face eased his tension a bit. "I want to see your wings, Kabril."

My wings?

At any other time he would have attempted to reason with her, make sure she was ready to see him shift forms, but his resolve was weak. He let go, allowing feathers to emerge on his upper shoulders first and then his shoulder blades. One barely there pinch later and his wings unfurled. A blanket of brown, white and gold enveloped them as Kabril extended his wings out and around them.

Rayna squealed and touched one of his wings tentatively, as if she was afraid she would cause him pain. Her touch had the exact opposite effect. Pleasure shot straight through his body, settling in his cock each time she touched his wings. He bit his cheek, trying to focus on anything other than the fact he was close to paradise. "R-Rayna," he ground out. "Do you accept me—all of me from now until the end of time?"

"Yes, Kabril. Yes."

With that, he surged forward, sinking his cock into her silken depths and relishing the feel of his mate's body encasing his own. Her pussy held him to her. She was tight. Made just for him.

The base of his spine tingled and Kabril knew additional feathers were forming on his back. He also knew his magik was rising, preparing to share itself with her, granting her the ability to live as long as him.

"Uh, Kabril," Rayna panted as he began to slide in and out of her. She clung to him, countering his thrusts and rubbing her body against his. Her pussy clenched around his cock as Rayna tipped her head back. "I'm coming. Kabril, yes!"

Liquid warmth made their already glorious merging even better. His magik picked then to rise, circling them with static-charged energy. Rayna continued to come, paying no mind to the power around her. For

Kabril, the moment was momentous. Never before had he shared his magik with another. Doing so during the act of coupling forever bound Rayna to his heart and his soul. They were as one now. Should one die, the other would follow shortly thereafter. She was now, in the eyes of his people, his wife, his mate, his queen.

He exploded, rooting himself deep within her core as his cock twitched, jetting forth seed. Kabril's entire body shook from the force of it all. The intensity was unlike anything he'd ever experienced. His cock remained hard, even after his seed was spent.

Wrapping his arms around Rayna, Kabril captured her mouth with his as he used his extended wings to lift them from their current position. Rayna yelped and held tight to him.

Chuckling, Kabril slid his hands down and cupped her ass. "Ride me, *ta'konima.*"

She glanced down, looking uneasy.

"Worry not. My power helps in keeping us afloat. We will not fall."

Rayna nodded, biting her lower lip and driving him mad with desire. She began to move her hips slowly at first, before working into a faster rhythm. When she varied her movements, moving up and down on him, Kabril seized hold of her and started impaling her on his cock.

Cries, moans and animalistic grunts broke free of them both. The smell of sex filled the air and Kabril's magik still buzzed around them. The moment was perfect and worth waiting four hundred cycles for.

Rayna's pussy milked his cock as her legs tightened around him. He knew she was coming and wanted to join her. He pumped feverishly into her, savoring the feel of his mate. His sac drew up a second before he expelled his seed, filling her with all he had to offer.

"*Ta'konima,*" he whispered, nuzzling his face into the crook of her neck and planting kisses there.

A sultry laugh bubbled up from her. "Mmm, tell me what *ta'konima* means."

"It means 'my love' in my language. *Ta'konima* from a man to a woman and *to'konimo* from a woman to a man." He kissed her again and she stiffened. "Rayna?"

"You love me?" The question, while so innocent, nearly broke him. How could she not know what he felt for her? How could she not see what he'd done?

Because you have not told her and she knows not your ways.

"Yes, Rayna. I love you. I have loved you since you took me to see your Henry. Each day I fought the urge to lay claim to you." He expelled a long, tired breath. "I could wait no longer."

"Lay claim to me?"

He eased them back onto the bed and withdrew from Rayna. "What happened between us means, in the eyes of my people, you are my mate. Umm, my wife. I know it is not the same for humans. Sachin explained their customs to me, but what transpired, the sharing of my magik and our bodies, makes you queen to my people, Rayna."

Kabril waited for her to explode in anger. When tears arrived, he wasn't sure what to do. "Rayna, are you in pain?" Guilt consumed him. "I was selfish, taking you when you were not yet fully recovered."

"Shhh." She pressed her hand to his mouth. "I love you too, Kabril."

For a moment Kabril felt as if he had been struck senseless. The sound of his heart pounding filled his ears and his breathing increased. "You love me as well? You are not vexed by my…"

"Shut up with the vexing and kiss me, King." She pulled him to her.

Kabril laughed as he drew his wings back into his body, leaving no trace of them behind. He rolled, putting Rayna on top of him so he could stare up at her beauty. "I will cease my blathering if you commence with the games." He waggled his brows and Rayna blushed.

"The games, huh?" She raked her nails down his chest lightly.

"Mmm, I think I can come up with a few things, *to'konimo.*"

CHAPTER TWENTY-FIVE

Rayna woke to an empty bed. She sat up slowly, wondering where Kabril was. Her feet made contact with the cool floor and she shivered. She considered returning to under the covers but there was a gnawing at her stomach. She needed to find Kabril, though, she wasn't sure why.

Something was wrong.

"Kabril?" she asked, loudly than one would think necessary since it echoed throughout the chamber.

No response.

"Kabril?" She found a long white nightgown of sorts and slipped it on. She pulled her hair through the back and then peeked her head into the room adjacent to the one with the bed. A bathroom the likes of which she'd never seen before was there. And it was also empty.

Sighing, she went to the heavy door and pulled it open. She looked into the hall and wondered if the castle was always so vacant. Rayna walked the length of the long corridor, tapping lightly on each door on the way before opening them.

All empty.

Very strange.

She turned the corner, as she neared the stairs and nearly collided with a young girl, dressed like something from the past. The girl held a candle in one hand. The girl gasped and attempted to lower herself nearly all the way to the floor.

"What are you doing?" asked Rayna.

"My lady," the girl said. "My apologies. I did not see you there."

Rayna nearly laughed. "Up. Please."

The girl did as asked but didn't meet Rayna's gaze.

"Kabril," Rayna said. "Where is he?"

"My lady, you should rest. He will be back soon. When he is done."

The pit in her stomach seemed to grow. "Done doing what?"

The girl appeared very nervous. She kept glancing at the staircase. Rayna's heart sank. Was the man she'd given her love to with another woman?

No.

He wouldn't.

Would he?

"Is he with another woman?" she asked, her voice small.

The girl squeaked. "No! He is in the lowest level of the castle—" The girl slapped her hand over her mouth and shook her head. "I never told you. Please, my lady."

Rayna touched the girl's shoulder. "You *never* told me."

The girl hurried off and Rayna started down the seemingly endless stairs. She couldn't explain the burning need to find Kabril. It was twofold. She felt as if something horrible was about to happen and in addition to that, she simply wanted to be near him.

It was strange the way she already ached for him as if they'd been separated for some extended period, rather than just a small bit. She missed the feel of him. Missed knowing he was close to her and more than anything missed the feel of his powerful arms wrapped around her body.

Finally, she reached what she could only assume was the staircase to the lowest level. She started down it, noting it was steeper than the other stairs had been and not as well lit. Recessed portions of the wall held sconces. A candle burned in each one, doing very little to pierce the darkness. A dark runner ran the length of the hall, keeping her bare feet from padding against stone.

The moment Rayna heard voices, she quickened her pace, bounding down the steep stairs at a speed she shouldn't have. She tried and failed to come to a stop at the bottom. Instead she slid on a slick, cold floor and crashed shoulder first into the wall.

The sound of Sachin's voice caught her attention, making her ignore the pain shooting through her arm. His voice was faint but unmistakable and he did not sound pleased.

"My lord, mayhap he speaks the truth."

"He lies!" Kabril shouted, his voice so deep and dangerous that it vibrated around her. The ache in her stomach grew and she knew without a shadow of a doubt that her man was about to do something she would not like in the least. "The knave spouts venom from his lips with his deceit. My queen would never rush to the aid of my enemy."

Aid of the enemy? His queen?

The sound of something cracking grabbed her attention. She followed the noise and tripped over the edge of a heavy wooden bench. Rayna put her arms out, in hopes of catching herself and ended up grabbing hold of a wall sconce. It turned, lever-like, and the stone wall nearest her opened, revealing another damn staircase.

Sachin's voice became clearer. "My lord, ask the queen."

This time it sounded as if something snapped. The noise was followed by a painful cry and Rayna recognized the voice immediately—Lazar. She ran down the steep steps and when she came to the end she covered her mouth, unable to believe the sight before her.

Kabril cracked a whip and it bit at Lazar's exposed chest. Lazar's wrists were bound above his head as he hung, suspended from iron chains. Blood trickled down him as his chest heaved. Rayna's gaze traveled the length of the large room. A cornucopia of torture devices lined it. With her mouth agape, she stared at Kabril horrified by what she was seeing.

His black hair clung to his sweat-soaked face. The feral look in his eyes made her take a step back as he gritted his teeth, his attention still

109

solely on Lazar. "You dared to harm my mate. To take her from me and leave her for dead. For this, you shall suffer my wrath." He drew the whip back again and Rayna dashed forward, putting her body between Kabril's and Lazar's.

Sachin was suddenly before her, shielding her with his massive body. "My lady!"

"S-Sachin?" she asked, her voice barely there. "What? Why?"

Sachin blinked and lowered his head, shame evident on his face.

Rayna trembled, her mind racing, words wanting to break free from her but they couldn't seem to get in sync with her head. She cupped her mouth, pushing past Sachin and rushing at Lazar.

Lazar shook his head, the action looking as though it cost him greatly. He winced in pain. "Go."

"No," she whispered, her heart pounding, confusion still gripping her. She twisted, keeping herself between Kabril and Lazar. "Why?"

Kabril's golden gaze burned with rage. The veins in his neck stood out noticeably. "He dared to harm you."

"No. He didn't."

Kabril continued to glare.

Finding her courage, Rayna put a hand on her hip and glared right back at him. "If you're going to shout orders at me or try to hit me with that whip, I'll have you know that I'll—"

Suddenly, Kabril dropped the whip and backed away, the fire draining from his eyes. "Hit you? Rayna, I would never raise my hand to you. Never."

"But you'd beat a helpless man?" she demanded. "One who tried to keep me safe from his own people?"

Kabril grimaced and tipped his head.

Sachin took hold of her shoulder. "Explain. Tell him exactly what happened, Rayna, for his mind twists reality and truths, turning them into something more than they are."

She exhaled and continued to shake with adrenaline, fear and a hefty mix of rage. "I'm so hurt and mad at him right now I'd rather take that whip and crack him over the head than give him the benefit of the truth. He's too hard headed to hear it."

"Well, there is always that option," Sachin said. "If you decide you want to whip him, I shall hold him for you."

Kabril cringed. "Rayna, my love."

"Shut up," she snapped.

He blinked.

Sachin snorted.

Even Lazar seemed surprised.

She squared her shoulders. She'd tell them exactly what happened and then she'd demand to be taken home. "Yes, Lazar is who took me from the campsite."

Kabril's hand tightened on the whip.

Rayna leveled her gaze on him. "But, when he found out Kabril was a big fat liar and had done nothing but keep me in the dark for months on who and what he really is, Lazar decided I'd been through enough."

Now it was Kabril who refused to meet her gaze.

She bobbed her head, her anger still coursing through her veins. "And, I don't think for a minute Lazar ever intended to hurt me. He was about to take me home when the other Falco Per-e-something or others arrived."

Sachin bit his lower lip as if he were trying to keep from laughing. "*Falco Peregrinus?*"

"Right." She nodded, adding, "The man you're beating killed one of his own men to keep me from being hurt, and I think he would have done the same to Humbert if I hadn't infected his wound with soil from Earth. Lazar had been suffering from the effects already and it was too much for him. He fell into the water and I went in after him." Rayna blushed. "After I kicked Humbert where it counts."

111

"Where it counts?" Sachin asked.

She centered her gaze on his groin and he winced.

"Yeah, it worked, so don't knock it."

A horrified expression came over Sachin. "I would never suggest anyone knock *it*. For that would be most painful. Knocking should not be done to any man's groin. Ever."

She groaned and tossed her hands in the air. "I give up. You're all weird. And right now, I want to smack the lot of you. Well, not Lazar. He's the only one who doesn't deserve to have some sense knocked into him."

Kabril continued to look away from her and she snapped her fingers, forcing his gaze to her. "Have anything to say for yourself?"

He grunted and shook his head. "No."

CHAPTER TWENTY-SIX

Kabril stood, listening to his mate talk of how Lazar had come to her aid. Guilt for having allowed her to be taken to begin with settled over him. Seeing the shame in Rayna's blue eyes as she shielded the Falco with her body didn't help matters any. He was king, it shouldn't make a difference what anyone thought of him, but it did. He cared what light Rayna viewed him in. And right now, that light was anything but favorable.

Truth be told, she looked a lot like she wanted to see him strung up by his toes. Or, perhaps his ball sac. He cupped them, slightly worried she might make an attempt on them.

Sachin tipped his head. "My lord, permission to remove the prisoner's restraints?"

Nodding, Kabril made an attempt to go to Rayna. Her glared halted his progress.

Rayna crossed her arms under her breasts, causing them to thrust forward. "Prisoner? How about a guest? I like the sound of that better. Yes, guest works for me. That is what we'll call him."

"Rayna, you cannot possibly think to—" The stern look upon her beautiful face silenced Kabril. She would not allow him to get off so easily. He knew that about her.

She tapped a finger against her arm. "I'm still mad at you for lying to me, Kabril. Don't think you're going to get on my good side by beating Lazar to a bloody pulp. Let him down, clean him up and see to his wounds. He needs a doctor and something to eat, not to be interrogated by you—you big giant jerk."

Sachin opened his mouth to say something and Rayna shot him a nasty look. "One word from you and I'll make you eat my famous chicken divan."

Gulping, Sachin put his hands up, signaling defeat.

Kabril's stomach churned at the thought of eating chicken anything. His long-time friend thrust him towards his mate as if he were scared of the woman. "For the love of the gods, see to your woman before she truly does clip our wings."

"Your woman?" Rayna quirked a brow as she stared at Kabril. "I'm sorry, but I'm anything but your woman right now."

He gave in to the smile wanting to come and went to one knee as Sachin had told him human males did in situations such as this. He took Rayna's hand in his and stared up into her blue eyes. "Rayna, you will marry me the way humans do."

"I don't even like you at the moment," she shot back.

Sachin cleared his throat and Lazar laughed under his breath. It certainly was a mess if the prisoner thought Kabril was wasting his time. Kabril thought hard about Sachin's instructions and realized he'd commanded Rayna instead of asking her. He decided to try again. "Uh, umm, Rayna, would you do me the honor of being my ball and chain?"

The anger washed away from her face and then laughter erupted from her. She tipped her head back and covered her mouth with both hands as she continued to laugh at him. "Ball and chain? Heaven help me. My man thinks that's a compliment."

"Be my chick?" he asked, hopeful he got it right this time.

Rayna laughed harder.

Kabril shifted awkwardly on one knee. "My sexy significant other?"

She closed the distance between them, snorting softly and shaking her head. He went to try another only to find her pressing her fingers to his lips. "Shhh, Kabril. Yes, I'll be your wife the way humans do it too.

114

But, first you're going to make our *guest* comfortable, apologize to him and thank him for saving my life."

His heart soared. He swept her off her feet and would have taken flight with her had they not been confined to the dungeon. His need to feel the wind on his face would have to wait for his cock needed attention first. The need to get her back to their chambers and make sweet love to her was too powerful to resist. The Oracle had chosen well for him. Rayna truly was his perfect match.

He would not tell the seers as much. They could think he was angry for a few hundred years or so. It would serve them right, meddling the way they had. And Sachin would get *his* when he found his mate. Kabril would be there to be sure she too was one would could clip his friend's wings if need be.

He looked to Sachin. "See to our guest."

Sachin didn't bother to hide his laugh. "Nearly choked on that one, didn't you, my lord?"

"I am sure he did," answered Lazar. "Thank you, Rayna."

She smiled at him, but it was weak. "I'm sorry he hurt you."

"I would have done the same if it were my mate," Lazar replied. "I would have done far worse."

There was a loneliness in the man's eyes as he spoke of his mate and Kabril had to wonder if tragedy had befallen his chosen one.

EPILOGUE

Earth, three and a half months later…

Kabril slid his arms around his wife and held her close, running his hands over her low, swollen abdomen. The life they'd created grew within her. Every moment since its conception seemed like a miracle to him, to Rayna and to the people of Accipitridae. Already the somber moods had lifted and the people rejoiced once more. A festival was in the works, the first in many years. It was to honor their union and the coming of their child. At least that is what the people claimed. Kabril suspected they were looking for a reason to celebrate after so many cycles of dwelling on the negative.

The threat of war was still imminent. Relations with the *Falco Peregrinus* were still nonexistent. Lazar's presence in the castle sparked controversy at first, but he was beginning to grow on everyone, including Kabril. Sachin insisted the Falco could be useful for establishing relations with the *Falco Peregrinus* in the future. Lazar seemed to think he would never be welcomed back by his own kind. Kabril tended to side with him on the matter. Lazar was always welcome in Kabril's kingdom.

The wind picked up, causing orange and yellow leaves to scatter about. Rayna sighed and leaned back into his embrace. "It's so beautiful, Kabril. I'm going to miss it."

He kissed her temple. "*Ta'konima*—my love, I have told you time and time again that you do not have to sell your grandmother's home."

She nodded. "I know, but we don't need it. We're keeping mine on the off chance one of your men wants to visit, and we live in

Accipitridae." She glanced over her shoulder at him. "Your castle sleeps about a hundred people or better, so I don't think we need this as a guest house."

"It holds sentimental value to you, Rayna." He rocked her gently, drawing in her sweet scent.

"I'll make new memories with you, Kabril. You're my family now."

He cringed, not wanting to broach the subject he needed to. "Speaking of family. You met my brother Rossi."

Rayna arched a dark brow. "Yes, and I still think you're too hard on him. But I don't think that's what you're getting at. What's up?"

"Word came of my other brothers arriving soon to welcome you to the family."

She licked her lips and grinned. "Are you going to tell me how many brothers you have finally?"

Kabril stiffened. "I have seven brothers. Two were born minutes behind me. There are two sets of twins. Then Rossi, he was a single birth."

One. Two. Three. He mentally counted down until Rayna's temper flared.

"You have how many sets of what?" Rayna spun around in his arms, her eyes wide in disbelief.

"There is more," he said, against his better judgment. "For our kind, multiple births have nothing to do with the female. Apparently, male shifters of our kind release a chemical in our sperm which encourages a high fertility rate. The chemical has been absent for some time as it is tied to our magik."

Rayna clutched his arms, her fingernails digging into his skin. "Are you trying to tell me there is a good chance I have more than one baby growing inside me?"

A sheepish smile swept over him. "Yes."

117

"And this is coming up this late in the game why?" she asked, tapping her foot.

"I love you."

Rayna batted her lashes and let out a soft sigh. "I love you too but if you don't start telling me important things up front, you're going to be sleeping in the birdhouse."

He cringed and she laughed. "Ah, my queen, you have my word, you know now all of my secrets."

The End

ABOUT THE AUTHOR

Mandy M. Roth grew up fascinated by creatures that go bump in the night. From the very beginning, she showed signs of creativity—writing, painting, telling scary stories that left her little brother afraid to come out from under his bed. Combining her creativity with her passion for the paranormal has left her banging on the keyboard into the wee hours of the night.

She's a self-proclaimed Goonie, loves 80s music and movies and wishes leg warmers would come back into fashion. She also thinks the movie *The Breakfast Club* should be mandatory viewing for...okay, everyone. When she's not dancing around her office to the sounds of the 80s or writing books, she can be found designing book covers for NY publishers, small presses, and indie authors.

Mandy writes for The Raven Books, Samhain Publishing, Ellora's Cave Publishing, Harlequin Spice, Pocket Books and Random House/Virgin/Black Lace. Mandy also writes under the pen names Reagan Hawk, Mandy Balde, Rory Michaels and Kennedy Kovit.

To learn more about Mandy, please visit www.mandyroth.com or send an email to mandy@mandyroth.com.

For latest news about Mandy's newest releases, subscribe to her newsletter

www.mandyroth.com/newsletter.htm

MANDY M. ROTH, ONLINE

Mandy loves hearing from readers and can be found interacting on social media.

Website: www.MandyRoth.com

Blog: www.MandyRoth.com/blog

The Raven Books: www.TheRavenBooks.com

Facebook: www.facebook.com/AuthorMandyRoth

Twitter: @MandyMRoth

Book Release Newsletter: mandyroth.com/newsletter.htm
(Newsletters: I do not share emails and only send newsletters when there is a new release/contest/or sales)

THE RAVEN BOOKS' COMPLIMENTARY MATERIAL

The following material is free of charge. It will never affect the price of your book.

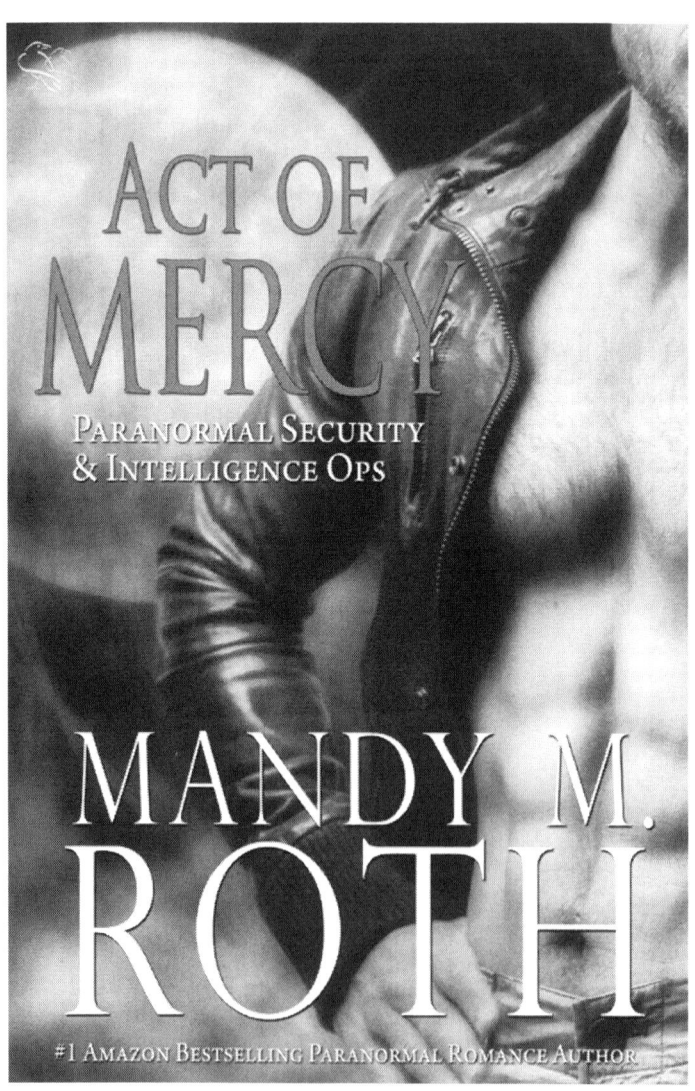

ACT OF MERCY

PARANORMAL SECURITY & INTELLIGENCE OPS

MANDY M. ROTH

#1 AMAZON BESTSELLING PARANORMAL ROMANCE AUTHOR

ACT OF MERCY
(PSI-OPS SERIES / IMMORTAL OPS)
BY MANDY M. ROTH

Book One in the PSI-Ops Series

Paranormal Security and Intelligence Operative Duke Marlow has a new mission: find, interrogate and possibly eliminate the target—Mercy Deluca. He knows looks can be deceiving, but it's hard to believe the beautifully quirky woman running around in a superhero t-shirt is a viable threat. The sexy little biomedical engineer quickly proves she is more than he bargained for and Intel has it all wrong—she's not the enemy. Far from it. Intel also forgot to mention one vital piece of information—she's Duke's mate. This immortal alpha werewolf doesn't take kindly to her being in danger.

When Mercy accepted a position within Donavon Dynamics Corporation, she thought it was to help cure disease and to make a difference for mankind. She had no idea what her new career path truly entailed—monsters masquerading under the guise of scientific research. Unable to stomach the atrocities she's uncovered, she reaches out through what she hopes is the proper channels, asking for help. Mercy gets more than she bargained for when a team of paranormal hotties show up on her doorstep ready to take down the Corporation. One in particular is able to get under her skin, both aggravating and exciting her in ways she can't explain.

EXCERPT FROM ACT OF MERCY

Paranormal Security and Intelligence Division B Headquarters,

classified location…

Duke Marlow stretched the two typing fingers he used because he wasn't exactly gifted in the way of a keyboard, and hunted and pecked the last of the reports that'd been due in to his handler—who also happened to be captain of his ops team—several days prior. With Duke's reluctance to do any type of recordkeeping, let alone the kind that involved a computer, his handler would be happy to see the files this quickly. Duke was actually at least one month early if anyone went off his past turn-in dates, or the fact that occasionally he never turned in a report at all. The idea of leaving the damn things to sit for a few more weeks had crossed his mind.

That would piss Corbin off for sure.

Corbin Jones headed one of the many Paranormal Security and Intelligence Operative Teams (PSI-Op) and Duke already knew he was Corbin's most trying team member. He wore the badge with honor. What could he say? After knowing the guy well over a hundred years, he had to do all he could to keep their working relationship interesting. Plus, Duke was set in his ways. He didn't embrace change.

Never had.

Besides, he enjoyed getting under Corbin's skin. Corbin was a lion shifter, and everyone knew cats and dogs didn't mix well together. As a full-blooded, born werewolf, Duke tended to get a kick out of giving Corbin as hard a time as possible.

Came pretty easy to him and that nearly took the fun out of it.

Nearly, but not quite.

And Corbin looked like a blond underwear model. That alone was grounds to be given a hard time.

The phone on his desk rang, drawing him from his thoughts. He sighed. He disliked the phones at PSI. Too many buttons. Too many options. It was never just answer and be done. They had people who normally handled routing the calls. Without them, Duke would be totally and completely lost. It was way after hours and he knew there was still a group who worked somewhere in the building, handling these types of things. What he couldn't figure out was why they'd send a call his way. Corbin had taken Duke's phone privileges away when he'd told a conference call full of people to get bent. He'd then followed that up with the suggestion they lick his balls.

Corbin hadn't been amused and said Duke lacked anything in the way of phone etiquette. Duke could have told him that to start with.

He answered the phone. Hell, the apocalypse could be starting and Duke suspected Corbin wouldn't want him getting called over it. "What?"

There was silence on the other end. Duke waited a fraction of a second and hung up the phone. He wasn't in the mood for bullshit. If it was important, they'd call back.

The phone rang again.

"What?" he practically shouted as he answered it again.

"Hello?" came a voice that was soft and sweet, extremely feminine and hot as hell, making his loins stir, surprising him. "I was told to call. Did you get the information I sent?"

As much as the voice moved him, its owner was making no sense. "What?"

"Do you know how to say anything else?" she asked, sounding annoyed with him. Most people tended to after short bursts.

He stiffened. "You called to give me crap? Striker put you up to this, didn't he?"

"Striker?" There was beeping on her end. "I can't talk long. They'll hear me."

"Woman, you're not making any sense." But damn if her voice wasn't making him hot and bothered. He was nearly ashamed of his reaction to her. It wasn't like he made a habit of getting a hard-on for random callers. The idea of phone sex had held little appeal to him before but now, hearing this woman's voice, he was fast changing his outlook on it.

"I need to know if you're them," she said.

"Them who?" As turned on as he was, he had reports to get done and the conversation wasn't going the route of phone sex so it needed to end sooner rather than later.

"Them. The one Test Subject 87P told me to send the information to," she insisted.

Great.

Sexy voice and bat-shit crazy. Just his luck. He hung up on her. Whatever game Striker was playing wouldn't work. Duke was busy. Too busy even for hot voices with riddles.

Duke rotated his neck, running his hands through his shoulder-length dark hair, working out a kink as he sniffed the air, the wolf in him catching the scent of pending rain.

Good.

The area needed some rain. He grinned, knowing he'd be running free in it soon enough. Well, as soon as he finished this damn paperwork. He didn't understand the point of it. It wasn't like the organization existed to anyone who asked about it—not that anyone even would. They were ghosts. Operatives who never were and never would be, at least on paper.

What the fuck did they want with a paper trail then? Did they enjoy redacting crap later? Maybe the guys who sat around drawing black lines through important information had blackmail photos of people in high positions and threatened to expose them if they didn't get enough papers passing across their desk.

Made no sense to him.

Not much involving the people running the PSI show did.

Seemed like they'd be keen on keeping no records. Records proved a lot. Immortals tended to avoid them, photographs and the like. It was getting harder and harder to hide in the open. The fucking internet was a curse as far as he was concerned. You wouldn't catch supernaturals taking pictures of themselves and posting them on the internet.

Most supernaturals took great care to reinvent themselves every so many decades. It threw off suspicions. He'd been the sole beneficiary of his own fortune several times over already.

Duke liked to reinvent himself, as far as the human public was concerned, every twenty to twenty-five years. That was as long as he could pull off not aging. That was hard. Most supernaturals kept it around fifteen years. Then, they'd go off the grid for just as many. In the beginning it had been hard knowing he'd never be able to see the human friends he'd made within that invented persona's lifespan. With time, it got easier and he found himself befriending fewer and fewer humans to avoid issues at a later date.

PSI gave him a network of supernaturals in like situations. That was part of why he stayed, despite the technology advances and dumbass higher-ups. He liked the good they did as well, but he'd rather everyone not catch on to that tidbit.

Do-gooder didn't fit his manly code.

It was simply easier to hang with others like him. He was young as far as PSI was concerned. And he was hardly a pup. Most of the people within the organization had been part of it a hell of a long time. Longer than any administration had been in control of the White House. From what Duke had been told, longer than there had even been a White House. They operated above the law and didn't answer to anyone but themselves. Certain people within positions of power in the government were on a need-to-know basis regarding PSI-Ops.

Most didn't need to know jack shit, so they didn't.

Duke liked it that way.

The ones in the loop were supernaturals, hiding in the open in front of humans. Duke nearly laughed at the thought of it all. He'd seen enough humans freak out over the course of his lifespan to know they couldn't take the truth. Hell, they couldn't handle much at all, let alone knowledge of immortality.

Immortality.

The idea would lead one to think of eternal life. Of invincibility. Nah. That wasn't how it was. It just meant an immortal was harder to kill and tended to live a lot longer than a mortal. Enough of his family and friends had fallen to know they could be killed.

Time and volume did nothing to lessen the losses. And there always seemed to be more losses ready to pick open the scabs of the old ones.

He hated people who died.

Hated them.

The phone rang again and Duke's already thin temper wore through. He snatched the receiver up and put it to his ear. "What!"

"Please, I need to know if you're them," came the sexy-as-all-get-out voice.

His nostrils flared. "Woman, this is a private line reserved for shit you can't possibly wrap your mind around. Stop using it for your crazy."

"I'm not crazy."

"Oh, you just go around talking about test subjects all the time?" he asked. "Let me guess, you were taken by aliens who did naughty things to you."

"I'm sorry, what?" she responded, huffing.

"Hey, if it's an anal probing you're after, I'd be happy to volunteer."

"You are a pig," she shouted back.

"No. I'm a wolf. So, is that a yes or no to the anal probing?" Damn, she had a hot voice and he'd love to have her bent over before him. His dick throbbed at the idea.

"Jerk!" she yelled before hanging up on him.

Whatever.

To find out more about these books or to read other books from The Raven Books visit www.TheRavenBooks.com

The
IMPATIENT
Lord

MICHELLE M PILLOW

The
DRAGON
Lords

THE IMPATIENT LORD (DRAGON LORDS)
BY MICHELLE M. PILLOW

Bestselling Dragon Shifter Romance

An unlucky bride…

Riona Grey lives life on her own terms, traveling wherever the next spaceship is flying and doing what she must in order to get by. When her luck turns sour, she finds herself on a bridal ship heading to a marriage ceremony. A planet full of dragon shifters seeking mates wasn't exactly what she had in mind as a final destination. Just when she thinks things couldn't possibly get worse, she wakes up months later in an isolation chamber with a sexy, hovering dragon shifter by her side telling her they're meant to be together…forever.

The impatient groom…

After years of failed marriage attempts at the Breeding Festivals, the gods finally revealed Lord Mirek's bride…a day too late. Eager to have her, he defied tradition and laid claim. But it is a mistake to go against the gods and his new wife was the one to pay the price of his impatience.

Now almost a year later, his bride is finally waking from her deep sleep. With one look from her, he feels the eagerness to claim her overtaking him once more. Fearful she'll slip through his grasp once again, he's hesitant to anger the gods by taking her to his bed too soon. But, how can he resist the one thing that would make his life complete, especially when she looks at him with eyes of a seductress? This is one test he can't fail, and yet with one of her sweet kisses he knows he may already have lost.

THE IMPATIENT LORD EXCERPT

"What happened to you?" Alek eyed Mirek in concern. "Did you have to wrestle negotiate with the Syog again?"

"My wife." Mirek stopped his slow, ambling walk and leaned against the corridor wall. Not that he would complain, but Riona had taken to intimacy with a vivacious force he'd ever dreamed possible. "She's, ah, fully recovered now."

Alek quirked a brow. It took him a long moment to understand what was happening. His concern turned into hard, full laughter. He clutched his stomach and bent over, struggling to breathe.

"What's going on out here?" Bron appeared from the scroll room, holding a stack of yellowed parchments. He eyed his brothers curiously.

"Lady…learned…sex…balls," was about all of Alek's answer they could understand.

Mirek grimaced. He should have known better than to admit soreness to one of his brothers. Why hadn't he lied and said he'd been getting his privates kicked in a Syog ball racking negotiation? It would have been an easy lie. Those aliens were rough on the manhood, even if they used a semi-protective plate. No one would have questioned his claim. They would have still laughed at him, but they would have believed him.

"Mirek?" Bron asked in concern.

"Riona, ah—" Mirek began.

"He can't handle…his wife," Alek interrupted in merriment. "He's walking like this." Alek ambled around the hall like an old man with a cane, stumbling all the more in his fit of laughter.

Bron arched a brow and nodded his head. "Nicely done. We'll have another nephew to add to the family soon. Well done, brother."

"If she didn't break him," Alek inserted. "I always suspected you were a little soft, Ambassador. All that flying in space and drinking lady wine with the aliens."

Mirek shoved Alek into a wall. It didn't stop the laughter as the man slid to the floor. "At least I don't smell like a ceffyl herd."

"I deserve that," Alek admitted, not bothering to stand as he grinned up at them. A change had come over him since his marriage. He was happier and smiled more. Whatever Kendall had done to her husband, she'd managed to tame the stubborn man.

"You're going to tell everyone, aren't you?" Mirek sighed, not really worried. His wife wanted him. That was a good thing. Actually, she wanted him...and wanted him...and wanted him...and—

"Oh, yeah," Alek nodded. "Everyone."

"Alek," Bron broke in. "Maybe we should keep this to ourselves. If my wife is any indication of how the women were raised, her sister will not like being talked about in such a way. She will consider it insulting."

Alek instantly agreed. "Of course, I didn't think of it like that. I would never gossip about my sisters if it made them uncomfortable."

"Thank you," Mirek mouthed. Bron nodded once.

"Have either of you seen the updated communications plans?" Bron asked, nodding at his armload. "We're having a hard time locating some of the buried mountain lines to see if they're salvageable. Aeron wants to get the construction plans finished before the baby arrives and keeps asking if they're lines or transmit boosters. I honestly have no idea how they work."

"Why don't you just grab a line on one side and pull?" Alek asked, shrugging. "See where it leads. If it doesn't lead anywhere, I'd say we have transmit boosters. I don't know what a transmit booster looks like, but we can send the boys out to look for one in the trees or wherever."

"Apparently checking the line that way will take longer. Aeron ordered a ground imager but it won't be here until after the baby comes. She is *very* focused on getting this done. Now." Bron looked at them hopefully, an almost desperate plea on his face as he wanted to please his pregnant wife. "So have you seen the updated plans?"

"Updated as in the ones from fifty years ago?" Mirek frowned. "Did we even have plans? I don't ever remember seeing them. I seem to remember Sper just making it work. He'd go out with tools and come back later with everything working again."

"Alek?" Bron prompted.

"No clue," Alek said. "I think Sper kept all the plans in his head. When he died, he took the information with him. Though, come to think of it, after he died the network stopped breaking down so much. I wonder what that man was doing?"

"Intergalactic transmissions," Mirek answered. Sper never married, never even tried to marry. He was a very rare exception to the Draig culture in that way. "Something he called moving, moodies, movies?"

"Blast!" Bron frowned. "That's what I was afraid of. Aeron is not going to be pleased. She is a very organized woman." To Mirek, he said, "She was always like that, but it's getting worse. At first, she just arranged clothing in the closet according to styles and color. But then I caught her trying to alphabetize your giant trade agreement reports in my office in the middle of the night."

"Wait until your bride starts hiding your favorite throwing knives," Alek said. "I wish Kendall would merely reorganize reports."

"I believe that is part of the joys of pregnancy," Mirek offered. "I'm told women do that kind of thing."

"Kendall is doing many strange things. When I threw a couple knives in the house she scolded me for ruining the wood on the new throwing post. Then she tried to take away all the sharp objects and put them really high in the home so not even I could reach them. How's it going to be a throwing post if I can't put weapons in it and soften it up for my boy to learn? And how is my son going to reach the weapons if they're glued to the ceiling? You'd almost think she didn't want the child to have a sharp blade." Alek took a deep breath and lowered his voice to a near whisper. "Then, as I'm rubbing her wonderful giant belly and tell her I want at least thirteen children, she tried to hit me with a plate of chocolate and an ore sample she was looking at. My Kendall is not a violent lady."

The fathers-to-be shook their heads, completely at a loss.

"One visiting dignitary told me he and his wife called it nesting," Mirek said. "Toward the end time women start doing strange things to the home. They can't help it. You should probably help them. I don't like the idea of my pregnant sisters climbing high and lifting heavy objects. They seem a little off balance of late when they simply walk down the hall."

"Like a baldric slaughtering prey to make nest bedding," Alek concluded. "That actually makes complete sense. Perhaps that is why she is putting the knives up high. She's building a nest."

"Nesting. Aeron has been taking all the covers and pillows and surrounding herself with them at night. And quite frankly, some of the strange things she's been eating resemble food a baldric might enjoy— not in taste so much, but it looks disgusting. I think you may be right, Mirek. We should find a way to help them with this nesting process." Bron shared a determined look with Alek.

"At times like this I miss our mother. She would have told us what to do," Mirek said.

"How hard can it be to build a nest?" Bron's bearing seemed lighter than before. "Mirek, thank you. I'm glad someone in this family understands these women things."

To find out more about these books or to read other books from The Raven Books visit www.TheRavenBooks.com

A King's

RANSOM

MASTERS OF PLEASURE

REAGAN HAWK

A KING'S RANSOM
(MASTERS OF PLEASURE)
BY REAGAN HAWK

(pen name of Mandy M. Roth)

Book One in the Masters of Pleasure Series

On a quest to find his brother, King Kritan of Katarius on the planet of Panucia finds himself ambushed, beaten, tortured and then sold to fight in the arena games. The people of Tamonius—his rival kingdom—condone slavery, take public sex to new lows and try to turn a profit off anything they can. Nothing can change his hatred for everything Tamonius... That is, until he meets the most breathtakingly beautiful woman he's ever laid eyes upon. Surina of the House of Argyros, daughter to a powerful senator, stirs the beast within him, making it want to lay claim to her as badly as the man does.

Free or not, Kritan is a master of seduction, and has selected Surina as his newest prey. But this virginal beauty has secrets of her own—ones that change everything. And destiny just might have the last laugh.

Mandy M. Roth

EXCERPT FROM A KING'S RANSOM

City of Vesta in the Kingdom of Tamonius on the Planet Panucia...

Kritan of Katarius walked through the streets of Vesta, a city known across the planet for its corruption and wickedness. He drew his black cloak around him more—to hide the sword at his side and the dagger in the top of his left boot. The clothing he wore was appropriate for the area, though nothing he'd normally want upon his body—the material was something a commoner would wear and not to his liking. He preferred trews to the tunic with a roped belt. He liked his boots, not the ones he wore now that were more of a sandal, leaving some of his foot exposed. He disliked, too, the ring that held his sword, preferring his sheath. He had not dared to bring his personal sword and shield. They were things that would give his origins—and his role—away.

It was important to blend. At least for now.

Cool wind from the north, from across the Ice Seas, blew past him. It was welcome against the heat of Tamonius's summer. Kritan preferred slightly cooler weather. While he could warm his body naturally by allowing his beast to rise, he could not cool it as easily.

His lip curled at the sight of three women standing, their breasts hanging out of the tops of their tunics. They were whores. His homeland, Katarius, was not without pleasures of the flesh, but they did not openly display their sexuality as the people of Tamonius did. While Katarius had whores, the guards there policed the streets better, making sure the women who charged were corralled into taverns or brothels, not left to wander the streets aimlessly for any and all to see. So far Kritan had lost count of the number of women he'd seen since entering the walls of Vesta who were selling their bodies for a few measly coins or even stale bread. Such a state of things. And the Tamoni thought they were so superior to the six occupied countries on their home planet.

Kritan walked with his head up, moving with purpose, though he was not yet sure of where he needed to be. His informant had spoken of a tavern four roads within the gates of Vesta. As Kritan walked the length of the fourth row, he could count at least five taverns directly around him, each filthier than the last.

Unease settled over him. He had known this would be a fool's mission. One he should not have undertaken himself, but he'd had no choice. He had to find his brother. He had to make amends, and he would walk through the cesspool called Vesta a thousand times over if he thought it would give him a chance to make things right. Banishing Jaelyn all those years ago had been a mistake. One he'd lived with for nearly two decades. Lies and a woman—a woman Kritan had believed meant more to him than she did—had fostered an environment that left him speaking words he could not take back, and sending his brother far from home. So long had gone by with no word on his brother's whereabouts, that when a missive arrived telling a tall tale—one that spoke of Jaelyn not only being alive but in grave danger, so much so that his brother was suddenly on borrowed time, Kritan could not stop himself. He'd mounted a steed and set forth on a quest to find the man—to hell with the cost. Regardless that he had men to do such things for him. That, as King of Katarius, rushing alone into the kingdom of Tamonius was not simply reckless, it was suicide. This was his brother and he would right the wrong he'd committed long ago.

"You look like you like it rough," a whore said, cupping her unimpressive breasts as she wiggled for him. It was clear to see the woman had serviced many cocks in her days and life had not been kind to her.

Her friend and fellow whore slinked her arms over the woman's shoulders and flicked her tongue, as if being offered a threesome would create a more appealing sight for him to behold. Kritan was no stranger to threesomes, foursomes and more. But he would never soil himself with the likes of these women. All the face paint in the kingdom could not hide the signs of disease on their skin, and the reek of strong spirits they'd been drinking could not mask the fact they had not bathed in months. Maybe more. Both looked heavily used and past their prime. Neither motivated his cock.

He had been too long between fucks and should have felt his beast stirring, wanting release. As a Katarian male shifter he was immune to the diseases that plagued the non-shifters—sexual or not. Though dirty whores never tempted him. He had certain standards, ones belonging to a king. There were many women who begged to be at his service within his castle, ready to ease his cock should he but click his fingers. All were screened by him before being granted such a coveted position. And sometimes, when he felt randy, he would sneak away to the buttery with a serving wench or two.

Regardless how long it had been since he'd fucked, his focus remained firm—find his brother.

Find Jaelyn.

Nothing else mattered.

To find out more about these books or to read other books from The Raven Books visit www.TheRavenBooks.com